DIRTY TACTICS
SPECIAL WEAPONS & TACTICS 1

PEYTON BANKS

CONTENTS

Chapter 1	1
Chapter 2	9
Chapter 3	17
Chapter 4	25
Chapter 5	32
Chapter 6	40
Chapter 7	51
Chapter 8	61
Chapter 9	71
Chapter 10	81
Chapter 11	93
Chapter 12	105
Chapter 13	115
Chapter 14	127
Chapter 15	137
Chapter 16	145
Chapter 17	156
Chapter 18	164
Chapter 19	173
Chapter 20	183
Epilogue	190
A Note From the Author	195
About the Author	197
Also by Peyton Banks	199

Copyright © 2018 by Peyton Banks
Editor: Emmy Ellis with Studioenp
Cover Design by Studioenp

This is a work of fiction. Names, characters, organizations, businesses, events, and incidents are a figment of the author's imagination and are used fictitiously. Any similarities to real people, businesses, locations, history, and events are a coincidence.

All rights reserved.

No part of this publication may be reproduced, distributed, or transmitted in any form or by any means, including photocopying, recording, or other electronic or mechanical methods, without the prior written permission of the publisher.

"When love is not madness it is not love."
— **Pedro Calderón de la Barca**

1

The tension was thick in the air. Mac willed his heart to slow down as they approached the brick apartment building. His MP5 was comforting to him—he aimed it well. His team, Team Alpha of the Columbia SWAT, was one of the best in the state of South Carolina.

Today, they were infiltrating a well-known crack house and they were to obtain a notorious drug dealer that, according to a trusted informant, would be in the building today.

Sergeant Marcas MacArthur was leading his men into this building to safely secure the premises and obtain the target. SWAT officers were trained for high-risk situations such as serving a warrant for a dangerous target.

Together, the four-man team trailed behind each other without making a sound. Brodie, his entry man, was in front of Mac with Declan and Ashton pulling up the rear. They approached the door with Mac issuing hand signals for Declan and Ashton to move to the opposite side of the doorframe. All men were ready to breach the building, decked out in their black tactical gear with SWAT brandished on their ballistic vests.

The other three members of their team were posted outside. Myles, the sniper, would be posted with his rifle drawn and ready, if needed. Zain and Iker were located out back to cover the rear door should the target try to escape.

Mac's eyes met those of Declan's through his dark goggles. Their faces were hidden by their black masks, leaving only their eyes visible through their goggles. Their bodies resembled shadows in their protective gear, their weapons dark shapes.

As members of such a team, there was a blind trust between all members. They went into highly dangerous operations almost daily and had to know that they could trust each other.

He signaled for his men to hold to allow Brodie to use the ram to burst open the door. Mac would enter first with Declan and Ashton falling in behind him. Brodie would enter last, covering their backs as he entered the building. They had practiced this entry hundreds of times and had it down to a science. He tightened his grip on his weapon as Brodie turned and nodded, signaling he was ready.

They all watched him draw back his ram and swing it, slamming open the door with one mighty blow. Mac instantly flew into the room with his assault weapon high, sweeping the area. He could feel his men behind him. He swept his gaze over the corner he was to clear and found nothing. Old furniture lined the space. Declan cleared the other side. They silently moved to the hallway. Communication would be the use of hand signals, and if separated, they would then use their communicators.

Screams echoed through the hallway where a rundown-looking woman stood frozen. The expression of fear shone on her face. Two men came up behind her, releasing curses and drawing their weapons from behind them.

"CPD!" Mac shouted, identifying their team. "Put your hands in the air!"

He really didn't feel like having to do the mountains of paperwork that would be required if he shot someone.

Instead of doing what he asked, the three turned and ran. The team pursued the targets as they'd practiced. They quickly moved through the building, guns up and eyes trained on them.

This was a dangerous situation. Targets with guns, running scared, could make an easy raid turn deadly.

Mac could feel Declan behind him as they took the

hallway the first man had gone down. He fit the description of the drug dealer they were after. The back entrance of the building was covered by the other members of their team, leaving him nowhere to run. They slowly made their way down the corridor, alert and fingers on the trigger as they crept forward.

Mac's heart raced with the anticipation of the hunt. Visions of his past life in the desert as a SEAL flashed before his eyes. He blinked, clearing his vision.

This wasn't Afghanistan.

He again tightened his grip on his MP5, getting comfort from his weapon. They came upon a room with the door slightly ajar. He slowed and motioned for Declan to hold.

He pushed the door open and found it to be an old office. He caught sight of another door inside. He pushed forward into the room, sweeping it with his eyes and weapon to ensure it was clear. Declan eased in as they both turned toward the door.

Mac slowly moved forward and reached with one hand and swung the door fully open.

"Don't shoot!" the guy hollered, kneeling on the floor of the closet.

"Throw your weapon on the floor and come out with your hands where I can see them," Mac growled. His weapon was aimed on the man while he did as he'd been ordered. The handgun slid across the floor.

Declan kicked it out of the way.

"Just don't shoot. I'm coming out," the man snapped. His beady eyes flickered between Mac and Declan, who both had their weapons trained on him.

"Come out and keep your hands where I can see them," Mac demanded again.

The man obeyed.

"On your knees and turn around," Mac announced.

The man complied and released a curse as Declan swiftly moved in behind him. Declan followed standard procedures in ensuring the drug dealer didn't have any other weapons on him.

Mac kept his weapon sighted on the man, and Declan zip-tied his wrists behind him.

"Clear." Ashton's voice came through his earpiece. "Other targets obtained and secured."

"Let's move through and finish clearing the building," Mac growled into the mic.

They would clear the building and ensure it was safe. He would only be satisfied once his team left and there were no casualties.

"Job well done," Mac announced to his team as they rode in the BEAR, their tactical armored vehicle. The spirits were high as there were no causalities, no need for deadly force, and the target was obtained.

This was why SWAT was needed. For a situation that could have turned deadly for untrained officers, it had been an easy raid for his men.

"We're still on for your house tonight, right?" Ashton called out, his grin wide.

Mac held quarterly barbecues at his home for his team. This was something he'd started years ago to reward his crew and give them a chance to hang out together and blow off steam. It promoted bonding amongst the men, and they all looked forward to it. They all were off call this weekend.

The bravo team would be on call and covering, which would allow his men to relax and rest.

"Beers have been chilling in the fridge for days." Mac nodded, and cheers and whistles echoed throughout the small cabin that housed them for the ride.

Conversation turned to grilling, food tips, and the items they were all bringing. Mac leaned back, pride filling his chest as he took in his unit. Just an hour ago, his men had been focused and highly armed, as if going into war on the streets of Columbia. Protecting the public was something that was ingrained in all of them.

Ashton Fraser, the funny man, had spent ten years on the police force before being accepted into SWAT.

He was an accomplished negotiator and had handled many hostage situations.

Brodie Gibson, the squad's entry man, had spent time in Special Forces, which gave him the perfect background to join SWAT when he entered the police force.

Myles Burton, their sniper, was another Special Forces recruit to the police force when he took to civilian life. His skills with a gun were unmatched by anyone.

Declan Owen, Mac's best friend, had banded with the team the same as Mac had. They had served together in the Navy. SEALs, they were. Both of them were highly trained in combat and had completed tours overseas together and had grown close over the years. Mac couldn't think of another person who he'd rather have in his group now.

Zain Roman and Iker Baldwin had served on the police force for years and made SWAT through hard work and perseverance.

His squad was top in the state. They had won many commendations from the state's governor and the mayor of the city.

"Hope the steaks are big and juicy. I can eat a fucking horse right now," Zain grumbled, rubbing his belly.

The men chuckled as Zain exaggerated his hunger.

"Don't worry. I made sure the butcher cut them just right." Mac nodded, his lips turning up in a small smile. He had ensured that he'd have plenty of food for his men. They deserved the best.

Cheers went around the cabin. He knew they would eat him out of house and home tonight, but he couldn't care less.

"We're going to have a good time. We get tonight and tomorrow off. Back on Sunday at 0800 hours." Mac nodded toward the group.

"Nothing but beer and football for me," Brodie announced, leaning forward to perch his elbows on his knees.

"Hear, hear!"

The plan sounded good to Mac.

It sounded damn good to him.

2

The sounds of music and laughter filled the air outside Sarena Rucker's house. She had moved into her home a couple months before and had met all of her neighbors except the one holding a party in his backyard.

The smell of delicious barbecue was flowing through her open windows, and her stomach rumbled. She was tempted to crash her neighbor's party just to grab a plate and chuckled as she stretched out on her couch. Tonight she was off work and would be a couch potato. She was sure if she wanted, she could call her best friend, Ronnie, for a fun night out on the town.

Not tonight.

Tonight, she wanted to drink her wine and binge on all her shows she was behind on.

But the smell of the food was calling her.

Okay, maybe she should eat food with her wine, but that would mean she'd have to get up and cook.

Not happening.

She grabbed her phone and placed a call to her favorite Chinese restaurant that delivered. Within seconds, her food was ordered with the promise of delivery in about forty-five minutes.

"This is going to be a perfect night," she murmured as she aimed the remote at her DVR and hit her first show. "Wine and dine myself tonight."

Her thoughts turned back to her party-throwing neighbor. Every time she saw him, she practically drooled. She was sure that any woman with a pulse threw herself at him. Why wouldn't they? He was extremely tall compared to Sarena's five-foot-four frame. Muscles on top of muscles that he always had on display when he cut his grass. She lived for Sundays when he was out in the yard topless with a pair of shorts on while he mowed his lawn.

Just thinking of him pushing the lawnmower caused a shiver to slide down her spine. His chest glistened with perspiration on sunny mornings. She wasn't ashamed to admit that a couple of times she'd slid her fingers between her moist folds and flicked her bean till she climaxed watching him.

Nope, not at all.

That's how hot her neighbor was.

Marcas MacArthur was downright sexy, and him being a cop just fulfilled her fantasies of him all the more. Her elderly neighbor, Janet, was the street gossip and had told Sarena all she needed to know about Officer MacArthur.

Ex-Navy. Cop. Single.

Now all Sarena had to do was work up the nerve to approach the man.

She looked over at her wineglass and noticed it was empty.

"Refill time," she muttered and swung her legs off the couch. She stood and walked into her kitchen, breathing in the mouth-watering smell of barbecue still making its way in through the window.

Nosey, she moved over to stare out into the backyard. Quite a few men stood around his patio. Smoke lingered in the air, but she was able to see the men were all muscular and tall. Her mouth dropped open.

"Maybe I should call Ronnie over here." She chuckled. She knew her best friend would have a heart attack with all the good-looking man specimens in her neighbor's yard.

She gazed around her kitchen to see what excuse she could use to step out into her backyard so she could get a better glimpse of her neighbor. Her gaze fell on her trashcan.

How about that? It was full. Now she wouldn't be a good homeowner, allowing her trash to be full, would she?

She glanced down at her clothes. Shorts that

stopped mid-thigh and a t-shirt that cut off above her belly button, showing off her smooth brown skin. She was thick and knew her curves attracted most men. She bit her lip, her confidence wavering as she thought of her neighbor. He was the epitome of fitness, while she was short, thick, and curvy.

Recently, she had started running to try to get in shape. She didn't want to lose her curves but wanted to ensure she was healthy.

According to Janet, he had his team over every few months or so. This must be what she had been speaking of.

She moved over and grabbed her trash, tying it closed, then opened her back door. She made her way over to her detached garage. She could instantly feel eyes on her as she walked barefoot across her yard.

Conversation at the party ceased.

She bit back a smirk and innocently placed her trash into her large garbage can that sat next to her garage. She knew Marcas was looking at her. She could always tell when she was out jogging that he watched her. Even the few times she had passed him when he was on his front porch, she'd felt his eyes on her.

Her nipples tightened, and she turned. Her breath caught in her throat, just imagining his eyes taking her in, and moisture collected within her folds. All of the men in his yard looked as if they were perfectly chiseled sex Gods, but she only had eyes for one of them.

She began the return trek to her back porch and put a little more twist in her hips as she walked. She flipped her dark curls over her shoulder and allowed her gaze to flicker over to the party.

Five guys were frozen in place, none of them hiding the fact that they were watching her. She ignored Marcas's gaze and met the eyes of one of the shorter men with blond, spiked hair. She threw him a bright smile before heading back into the house. She closed the door behind her, and her smile widened.

She had officially made her move.

Mac had locked his gaze on Sarena the minute she'd appeared in her back yard. He'd taken notice of the way his men looked at her, too. He bit back a curse at the hunger in their eyes. None of them had hidden the fact that they were openly watching her.

Sarena Rucker, with her beautiful bronze skin, deep dimples in each cheek, was a registered nurse who worked in the local emergency room. He made it his business to know his neighbors. She had moved in next door a couple of months ago.

His cock grew stiff just thinking of the times he'd

seen her out jogging. Her barely there clothes did nothing to hide her delicious curves. The swell of her hips was enough to bring a man to his knees.

He'd bitten back a growl at the smile she'd tossed Brodie's way. A new feeling crept up in his chest.

Was that jealousy?

Never before had he experienced it, but today, for some odd reason, his fist wanted to connect with Brodie's wide grin.

A whistle cut through the air as she went back into her home.

"Who the hell is that?"

"Mac, you've been holding out! When did that brown-skinned goddess move in?"

"Is she single?"

Questions immediately shot out from his team, and they began discussing Sarena.

Mac put his attention back on the grill and raised the chilled bottleneck to his lips, pulling a long swig from it. He tended to the grill, his thoughts still on his sexy neighbor.

"Her name is Sarena. She moved in two months ago, and yes, she's single," he answered unconsciously.

The conversation halted again. He turned his head and found all eyes on him. He shrugged and kept all emotion from his face.

"You've met her?" Ashton asked, his eyebrows raised.

"No. Ran a background check on her," he admitted, turning back to the grill. He could feel the stunned eyes of his team on him at his announcement.

"Really, Mac? You ran a check on her?" Iker chuckled. "That's bold."

"Have you ever heard of approaching your neighbor and just have a conversation with them to get to know them?" Zain asked, his eyebrows high.

"I'm not even surprised," Declan drawled from his position. He leaned back in his chair, resting his feet on the railing of Mac's deck. His friend knew him well. They were similar, and Mac knew that Declan had done the same with his neighbors. "Mac always needs to know everything about anyone around him."

Mac nodded in agreement. He had run background checks on all the neighbors. He wanted to truly know who he was living around.

Questions were thrown out from the guys. They were like a pack of wild savages circling around fresh meat.

"She's off-limits," he ordered.

Complaints filled the air, and he shook his head, turning back to his team.

"How do you get to make that decision for her?"

Myles leaned back against the railing with his beer paused at his lips.

"I'm your commanding officer. What I say goes," he growled, looking them all in the eyes. "Besides, good neighbors are hard to find. Don't need the likes of you sniffing around her and chasing her off."

Chuckles filled the air as he checked on the last of the steaks.

"Food is done," he announced, taking the steaks off the grill.

His team ambled to the oversized table. He needed to get their attention off Sarena and knew she would be temporarily forgotten once food was placed in front of his men.

He swiveled his gaze back to Sarena's house for a brief second before moving toward the long table on his deck. His eyes met Declan's as he made his way there. Declan raised an eyebrow, and Mac knew his friend read him.

Mac wanted his neighbor, and in time, he would have her.

3

Sarena rushed over to the nursing station of the emergency room. They had received the notification from the EMTs that they were bringing in a cop who had been shot in the line of duty. Tension was heightened in the emergency room as they waited for the injured cop to arrive.

Just the thought that the cop being brought in could be her neighbor had her heart seemingly lodged in her throat. Her team was ready and prepared. Even the physicians were waiting for their new patient to arrive.

The EMTs appeared, wheeling in a large man decked out in black, cursing to the high heavens.

A sigh went around the emergency room. If he was fussing and cussing, he'd be okay.

The EMTs pushed his gurney over to one of the stalls then drew the curtain, leaving the glass door open.

Samantha, one of the techs, disappeared behind the curtains to get first vitals. The curses grew louder as she made her way toward the cop. The EMTs came from behind the curtain

"Give us a second." Sarena motioned for the resident to hold off going over there. She strode to the area, determined to get him under control first. She had much respect for the boys in blue and would be damned if one would come in her emergency department causing a ruckus.

"I know you are not coming into my E.R, cursing and disrespecting my nursing staff," she barked as she flung the curtain back. Her gaze connected with the officer, and she made sure she showed that she wasn't afraid of him.

"No, ma'am," he growled, sitting up on the side of the gurney.

She moved near the gurney and motioned for Samantha to hand her the blood pressure cuff. "I got this, Samantha. Close the door behind you."

Samantha's eyes were wide with fear, and she backed away quickly and disappeared behind the curtain.

"Let me guess, you don't want to be here?" Sarena asked, cocking an eyebrow.

His scowl increased as he looked her up and down. She could see a bit of respect in his eyes since she wasn't backing down from him. She knew cops could be stubborn, but she wasn't going to take any shit from him and if she had to, she'd force him to allow her to take his vitals.

"I'm fine. The bullet hit me in the vest. Go save someone else's life—"

"You will stay where you are," a deep baritone voice sounded from behind Sarena.

Her heart leaped, and she paused.

"That's an order."

She turned and met the eyes of Marcas MacArthur. He was still dressed in his tactical gear. Her gaze took in SWAT brandished across his vest. His face still had smudges of black on it, and she itched to be able to reach up and rub it off.

He was even larger in life standing next to her. She swallowed hard while trying to hide his effect on her.

"Bed," she ordered, turning back to find the other cop trying to get off the gurney. She narrowed her eyes on him, still holding the blood pressure cuff in her hand.

He let loose a deep sigh and sat back down on the bed.

"I didn't need help," she said, glancing at Marcas.

"Sure you didn't." He snorted.

"Want me to leave?" The guy on the gurney made

to move again. His eyebrows were raised, and he looked between the two of them.

"So help me, if you move from that gurney again, I will strap you down," she threatened.

"Never had to have a woman threaten to get me in the bed before." The guy chuckled, a smile lighting up his features.

His face completely changed with the smile. She could instantly see the sex appeal and knew that some woman would instantly be infatuated with him. Unfortunately, it was the man behind her who had her gut tied up in knots.

"Watch it, Dec," Marcas growled.

A shiver slid down her spine at the sound of his voice dropping low.

"You, out!" She turned toward Marcas and pointed to the door.

He narrowed his gray eyes on her. Gray eyes that reminded her of the deepest steel. She lifted an eyebrow, not afraid of him either. She was used to her brother and his alpha ways and hard attitude. She didn't know what it was about men and their alpha ways, but not here. *She* ran the emergency room.

A whistle echoed behind her.

"I think she means business, Sergeant. If I didn't know any better, I'd say she could take us both on." Dec gave a quiet chuckle.

Marcas's eyes flickered to Dec first before settling back on her. As if deciding whether or not he could trust his man or her, he must have come to a final conclusion that she could handle his team member, as his head jerked in a nod.

"If he gives you any trouble, holler," Marcas said before disappearing from the room.

She turned back to Dec and blew out a deep breath. Her heart was racing, and she willed it to slow down. Marcas MacArthur dressed in his tactical uniform just gave her more ammunition for her dirty fantasies.

"You, shirt off," she ordered so that she could do her job.

"Yes, ma'am."

Mac made his way back to the waiting room. He knew that the whole team would want a report on Declan. Silence fell on the room as all eyes turned on him.

"How is he?" Zain asked.

"He's good. Causing trouble for the nurses, but he'll be fine," he announced.

"Why didn't you straighten him out?" Iker asked, a smirk on his face.

They all knew Mac never bit his tongue and was the alpha of the team.

"The nurse kicked me out," he admitted, scratching the back of his head.

All eyebrows rose at his admission. He caught the surprised looks that passed between team members.

"I would love to meet the woman who kicked Mac out of the room." Brodie chuckled.

His team relaxed back in their chairs as they realized Declan would be okay. The minute Mac had watched his friend fall to the ground after a target had jumped out of hiding and took a shot at him, he'd lost it.

Mac, usually calm and collected, was trained for these potential situations. Declan was like a brother to him. They had been to Hell and back in the Navy. Mac had easily aimed his weapon at the shooter and pulled his trigger, putting him down.

"If you must know, it's my neighbor, Sarena." He moved to stand against the wall to wait with the rest of his team.

"A woman after my own heart." Brodie groaned, collapsing his hand across his heart.

Mac bit back a scowl as he watched his team smile and crack jokes, the fear for losing a member dispersing. Soon they would have to go and debrief with the commander. Since there were fatalities in this situation, they would have to answer to their higher-ups.

He kept an eye on the door, thinking of the way Sarena had handled Declan. He was truly impressed that she hadn't backed down from his friend, who he knew could be an ass. Hell, Declan was known to be a damn bulldog, and she hadn't even flinched. He'd seen the respect in his friend's eyes. Declan even had the nerve to give him a nod of approval when she'd turned her attention to him.

He'd seen the flicker of recognition in her eyes when she had looked to him. Her tiny figure had him ready to slam his old friend on the damn gurney just so she could get what she wanted.

His cock thickened at the memory of her in her nursing scrubs.

He wanted her.

The scrubs fit her just right. There was no hiding her curves. Her height put the top of her head to just below his chin. She was the perfect size for him. He imagined bringing her into his arms and instantly had to push that fantasy from his mind.

No need to have an erection in a room full of his men and his gear still on. He cleared his throat and willed his cock to soften, but it had a mind of its own. It wanted to feel the slick tightness of Sarena's pussy gripping it.

His phone rang, and he released a curse. He pulled it from his pocket, seeing his captain's name flash across the glass screen.

"Mac," he answered. He could feel the eyes of his team on him.

The room grew silent as he took the call.

"How's Declan doing?" Captain Donald Spook's deep baritone voice came through.

"He's doing fine, sir," Mac reported. "Bullet hit his vest. He'll have one hell of a bruise but should be fine."

"Good. See to Declan and then get your asses down here for debriefing."

"Yes, sir."

4

Sarena relaxed on her porch with her feet perched on her banister. She just wanted to relax on this warm fall night. Nights in Columbia didn't get too cold this time of year. It was one of the things she loved about living in the south. Warm weather all year round.

She paused with her beer to her lips as the rumble of a motorcycle making its way down their quiet street grabbed her attention.

Marcas.

She took a long sip and watched him roll up into his driveway. His machine gave a loud roar as he revved it up. The sound of her soft music playing from her small radio was drowned out by the sounds of his bike.

Marcas shut the engine off and parked, then got off and turned in her direction. He made his way across his yard. She had to hold back a sigh, taking him in, his t-shirt stretched across his muscular frame, his jeans resting low on his hips He headed toward her yard.

Marcas reached her small white picket fence. It had been one of the highlights of the house when she'd purchased it. It was to be her American dream, owning a home with a white picket fence.

"Howdy, neighbor," she called out, a smirk on her lips.

He paused at her fence. "Evening," he replied. "May I?"

"By all means." She waved her glass bottle in the air.

He was asking for her permission to enter her yard. She laughed. It wasn't like that little fence would actually block him.

He drew closer, and she greedily took him in again. The soft glow from her front door cast him in just the perfect light. Her body awakened.

"Are you the neighborhood welcoming party?" she drawled. "I seem to have forgotten to get cash. Do you take credit? I swear Janet didn't have to hire a cop to come welcome me properly. She must have known I had a thing for men who wear uniforms."

She allowed her smile to grow on her lips. She didn't hide the fact that she was looking him over.

He released a snort and came up her few stairs.

"I came to thank you for taking care of my team member today." He reached out his hand.

She dropped her bare feet to the floor and stood, taking his hand. His warm hand engulfed her smaller one, and he introduced himself. "Mac."

"Mac?" She cocked an eyebrow at him. "Sarena. So I'm curious. What does 'Mac' stand for?"

She would play like she didn't know his name. Janet had been sure to make sure that she knew the entire street before she had even met her neighbors.

"Marcas MacArthur."

He pulled his hand from hers, and she instantly missed his warmth. A tremor traveled down her body, and she cocked her head back to look him in the eyes. He was so much taller than her, and she loved it.

"Marcas," she murmured, her eyes meeting his. "I like it."

"Well, I'm glad that my name pleases you." His lips curved up into a small smile as he studied her.

"So if you knew who I was earlier at the hospital, why are you just now introducing yourself to me?" she asked, crossing her arms in front of her chest. Her nipples had beaded into little nubs and painfully pushed against her shirt. She prayed he didn't see how he affected her. From the way his gaze dropped to her chest, she knew it was too late.

He knew.

She toyed with the chilled glass in her hand and waited for an answer. His eyes flickered to her small cooler that sat next to her chair.

"Help yourself."

He stepped over and snagged a bottle and popped it opened. She watched him lean against her banister and take a long pull from the bottle before his eyes met hers.

"Because I usually don't do this." He motioned to her with his bottle.

"Do what?" she asked, puzzled. She pushed her thick hair behind her ear as he appeared to finish his train of thought.

"Fuck my neighbors."

Her throat suddenly became dry at his bluntness. She took a sip of her beer to clear her throat. Butterflies fluttered in her stomach, and she returned his heated gaze.

"Oh, really?" Her voice grew husky, and she gripped the bottle tight, trying to hide the tremors in her hand. She didn't want him to know how he truly affected her. "And you're just so sure that we're going to have sex?"

His eyes locked on her, and she had to keep herself from fidgeting. The air between them became heavy with sexual tension, making it difficult for her to breathe. Moisture seeped from in between her folds.

The heat from his gaze had her body strung tight.

She wanted him.

Deep within her.

She knew they would be good together.

Too good.

She was afraid to say anything else for fear that her voice would crack.

"I figured we've been fighting the inevitable. I know you watch me when I'm out in my yard." He cocked an eyebrow at her as if daring her to lie and say she didn't.

She cursed on the inside. Apparently, she hadn't been as discreet as she'd thought she'd been when she watched him. She just hoped he hadn't figured out what she did sometimes *when* she watched him.

"Let me guess, you've never watched me?" she asked, growing bold. She had thought the other night when he had his get-together in his yard that she was a big girl and could handle him.

Now, with him a foot from her, she knew she was totally out of her league.

"Oh, I've been watching you. Every time I see you out jogging in your little workout shorts and sports bra." He stepped forward, stopping directly in front of her.

She had to tilt her head back to meet his eyes.

"Or when you go out with your girls with those

fuck-me heels on. I want you, Sarena Rucker. Naked, in my bed, waiting for my cock to slide inside your wet pussy."

She widened her eyes at his words. Her heart raced as he reached out and rubbed her bottom lip with his thumb. She was mesmerized by him and couldn't move. She waited with bated breath for him to lean in and kiss her.

"These lips," he murmured, glancing at her mouth, his eyes darkening. "I would love to see them wrapped around my cock."

Her core dripped from his words. It would only take one swipe of his tongue or finger and she would explode. Her skin tingled from his small touch.

"Um," she gasped, unable to form any clear train of thought. Images of him braced over her filled her mind. Everything he'd mentioned, she would die to have at that moment.

He trailed his thumb to her chin and paused.

"I will have you, Sarena. My cock will fill your pussy, and you will take me," he growled.

Her breaths were coming fast, and she leaned into his hold, mesmerized by his words. Her imagination was on overload, images of them together flashing before her eyes.

"Everywhere."

Her body screamed for him to take her now. She

wouldn't give a damn if he stripped her out of her clothes right there on her front porch and bent her over her railing. Her pussy ached to feel him deep within her.

He stepped back and downed his beer. He saluted her with the beer bottle and backed away from her. In shock, she watched him jog down her stairs and make his way to his yard.

With only words, he had her so aroused that she was ready to beg him to come back to finish her off.

Her feet were frozen in place. He arrived at his bike and didn't even look her way while pushing it to the backyard.

She knew she had been playing with fire and may get burned.

Burned wasn't even the correct term.

Her entire body had just been set ablaze by one Marcas MacArthur.

5

Mac knew one thing. He wanted Sarena. He was no longer able to hold back. He knew that his job wasn't easy for any woman to accept.

Loving a cop was hard.

Loving a SWAT officer was damn near impossible.

He was on call for twenty-fours a day with rare occasions off. He was always put in dangerous situations that most spouses had a hard time dealing with. Many women couldn't stomach the thought that one night they may get a call that their loved one might not return to them.

He'd come home from the Navy knowing that he wanted to continue his duty of protection of the public. Signing up for the Columbia Police Department was second nature. It only made sense for him to apply for SWAT once he'd joined the force and made his way up the ranks to commanding his own team.

Finding love just wasn't in the cards for him.

His job was to put his life on the line for civilians and his brothers and sisters in blue.

True SWAT put themselves in danger without a second thought, and he'd bled for his men.

He couldn't offer Sarena much. He wouldn't make her any promises. Maybe after they'd fucked a few times, he'd get her out of his system.

Who am I kidding?

One didn't get a woman like Sarena Rucker out of their system. A woman like her soaked into your pores and became a part of you. She was the kind of woman who could bring him to his knees.

And that scared him shitless.

He stared down at his cell phone as he sat back in his recliner in his living room. He'd gotten her cell phone number during the background check and had held on to it.

He sent her a quick text. *Dinner at my place tonight?*

Who is this? Her reply was almost immediate.

Mac.

His phone rang with her name flashing across the screen. He bit back a chuckle and answered it.

"Hello?"

"How'd you get my number?" Her husky tone came through the line.

His cock grew stiff at the sound of her voice. Last

night, when he'd approached her on her porch, his feet had moved on autopilot. He hadn't even known what he was doing until he had reached her porch.

Her soft caramel skin made his fingers itch to touch her. She'd been relaxed and well into a few cups. Had she not been slightly tipsy, he would have had her then. But no, he wanted to ensure she remembered their first, second, eighth time together.

"I have my ways." He leaned back in his chair, a small smile playing on his lips at her sass. He would love to draw out her feisty nature in the bedroom. Just imagining her flirting with him in nothing but her heels, on her knees in front of him, got him rock hard.

"So you are asking me out on a date?" she asked.

"I don't date," he automatically replied. He wasn't going to lie to her. He didn't date around. The women he had been involved with in the past had known what they were getting into with him. He knew that Sarena was different but he could no longer stay away from her.

"So just dinner?"

"I'm not going to lie to you, Sarena. I want you," he stated. He wouldn't sugarcoat anything with her. He heard the slight catch of her breath and wanted to ensure that if he was going to take this step that it would be on his terms.

A small shred of doubt entered his mind. Would

she turn him down? Would she prefer the likes of Brodie to him? The memory of her throwing his teammate a smile came to mind. She was probably looking for romance, flowers, and a happy ever after—the shit he didn't do.

He scowled knowing that those things weren't him. There was one thing he knew he *could* promise her—unbridled passion, screaming orgasms, and sexual satisfaction.

"What time do you want me there?"

Sarena's heart pounded away as she finished putting the last details on her makeup. She didn't want to put on too much and wanted to keep it light and natural. Tonight, Marcas had invited her over for dinner but she was sure there would be much more on the table than just food.

She glanced down at her watch. Fifteen minutes until she needed to be at his home. She blew herself a kiss, hit the light switch, and left her bathroom. Due to his confession on her porch, she knew he loved her in her heels so she'd ensure she wore a pair tonight.

She slid her feet into her shoes and moved to stand in front of her floor-length mirror. She kept her outfit simple since she was just going to his home and released a snort. If he had his way, her clothes wouldn't be on for long.

She didn't have a problem with that.

No, not at all.

The sound of the doorbell filled the air.

"Who could that be?" she muttered and made her way down the stairs. She wasn't expecting anyone and she knew that her best friend, Ronnie, had picked up an extra shift tonight. "Coming," she called.

She walked over to the front door and peeked through the peephole.

Marcas.

"Marcas," she breathed as she opened the door.

He stood there in a t-shirt that molded to his chest, displaying his well-defined muscles. His jeans hung low on his waist, and he leaned against her doorframe. His intense gaze made her breath catch in her throat.

"What are you doing here?"

Her nipples tingled while he perused every inch of her body, stopping at her heels. Her leopard-print heels were one of her favorites. His eyes darkened and met hers again.

He approved of her shoe choice.

"Well, I didn't want you to have to walk over to my place alone for our non-date dinner," he murmured.

"Our non-date dinner?" She raised her eyebrows. She smirked and crossed her arms in front of her chest, propping her door open with her hip. He could call it want he wanted, but it was a damn date. "Because you don't date."

"Nope, but I can feed my neighbor, though." The corner of his lips curved up in a faint smile.

"Because that's just what good neighbors do," she whispered and met his heated gaze.

His attention dropped down to the swell of her breasts that were on display from the low-cut shirt. Any place that his gaze touched had her body heating up. She bit her lip and stared at him. She wasn't sure she'd be able to make it through the damn dinner. Her fingers itched to tear his clothes off so she could have her wicked way with his god-like body.

She dropped her own attention down to the bulge in his jeans and bit back a groan. "Well, let me grab my keys, neighbor."

She turned and held the door open for him. He stepped across the threshold, and she ran over to the couch and grabbed her phone and purse. She spotted her keys on the table by her front door.

"I hope you're bringing your appetite," he announced as she made her way back to him.

Her gaze flew to his eyes, and his eyes darkened again. Had she mistook what he was speaking about?

Appetite?

For him?

Hell yeah, she was bringing it.

"For dinner? I'm starving." She chuckled.

They walked out the front door. She turned and quickly locked up then turned again, jumping back against the door.

Marcas was right behind her, trapping her between his hard body and the door. His finger tipped her chin up so she could look into his eyes.

"I wasn't talking food, but I do hope you brought your appetite for that, too," he said.

His finger brushed against her bottom lip, and her knees grew weak.

It didn't make any sense how her body was responding to his with just the slightest touch. She'd never had this instant, go-up-in-flames reaction to anyone before.

He didn't date but he wanted her.

Well, she wanted him.

She was a grown woman and could handle herself. She'd just have to ensure her heart was locked away in a steel cage because this man in front of her could hurt her.

Destroy her.

She pushed off the door, narrowing her eyes on him as she pressed herself to him. With his tallness and her shortness, they fit together perfectly. She was soft everywhere he was hard.

They were perfect against each other.

A growl escaped his lips, and he met her gaze. Her mind was made up, and she'd be willing to take the risk.

Two could play this game.

"Lead the way, Marcas," she breathed.

6

Mac looked across the table and figured he'd gone too far. It had been a while since he'd just cooked for a woman. Hell, he couldn't remember a time when he'd prepared a meal for a female who wasn't his mother. Latrice MacArthur was a lady who'd made sure her boys knew how to cook. He and his brothers, Stone and Lincoln, loved to get busy in the kitchen. All three of the MacArthur boys had gone into the Navy, but Latrice ensured that once out of the service they would be able to survive on more than fast food.

If asked, Latrice told anyone who would listen that she wanted to make sure her boys were a catch for a woman. Mac scowled thinking of his mother's routine speech that she gave about wanting daughter-in-laws since she wasn't blessed to have a daughter.

"This was just amazing," Sarena gushed and waved her hand over the table.

He wanted to provide her a solid meal and thought

that grilled salmon and mashed potatoes with a small salad would be sufficient. Sarena was not a woman who was ashamed of eating. He was pleased with the way she'd dived into dinner with such gusto.

"Thanks. It really didn't take that long," he murmured, wiping his mouth off with his napkin.

"I'm ashamed to say that I'm not the world's best cook. I can get by with the basics but nothing this extravagant."

Her bright smile met his eyes as he gazed across the table at her. Her dimples winked at him, and he could feel the stirring between his legs. She laughed softly, and his cock grew stiff.

Their conversation had been steady for the entire dinner. He was surprised at how much he had opened up to her.

"So was it just you growing up?" he asked, leaning back in his chair, knowing the answer. The private company he used to obtain background checks was always reliable. He would just pretend as if he didn't have a few pages' worth of information on her already.

"No, I have an older brother." She shook her head.

He paused. The background check hadn't revealed any siblings. Curiosity burned in his gut. Alarms went off in the back of his mind, and he sat forward.

"Really?" He couldn't admit to her that he had run a background check on her. He wanted her to volunteer information. So far, most of her what she had told him lined up with the background check. She was the assistant nurse manager of the emergency department. She was raised by her parents. Her father, Walter Rucker, was a high school science teacher, and her mother, Carol Rucker, was the high school secretary.

No mention of a brother.

"Harden is in the Navy. He's a SEAL. He actually reminds me of you." She shook her head again, her smile faltering. "It's been a few months since I've spoken to him."

Mac's mind raced. If her brother was older than her, then he was probably around Mac's age. If he was still in the Navy, then that would explain why he hadn't been on the check. Harden Rucker didn't want to be found. Anywhere. Not even to appear under anything linked to family.

"What team is he on?" he asked.

"Team three," she murmured.

Mac knew by the look in her eyes that he needed to change the subject. He recognized that look. It was the same one that came over his mother's face whenever either him or his siblings deployed.

"I'm sure wherever he is, he's safe."

A small smile returned to her lips, and she glanced back over at him.

"I heard you were a SEAL, too." She cocked her

head to the side. "I would ask if you know him, but then again, this world is much bigger than we think it is."

"I think Janet has been talking too much," he muttered, pushing back from the table. He didn't want to go down memory lane of his days in the service right now. He was a proud SEAL but was scarred too badly to open up that far on their first date—

Non-date dinner.

He wasn't sure how his nosey neighbor knew so much about him. Maybe he should have just asked Janet about Sarena or any of the other neighbors to find out information since she seemed to have a wealth of knowledge.

"Here, let me help." Sarena scrambled from her chair and gathered some of their dishes then headed into the kitchen.

"You are a guest in my home, I'll clear the table," he argued, following her.

"Nonsense." She laughed and placed the dishes on the counter and turned to him.

He lowered his into the sink then moved to stand in front of her. He settled his hands on the counter on each side of her hips, trapping her with his body.

"It's the least I can do," she said. "You cooked, I can clean."

He could see the feistiness come forth on her face, and she smiled up at him.

"You are a guest, Sarena. No cleaning up here," he murmured, shaking his head.

"But we are just two neighbors dining together, so I can help clean. This is not a date, remember?" She cocked an eyebrow at him and used her finger to tap him on the chest.

There it was again.

Her feistiness.

She was testing him.

He shot his hand out and grabbed her finger.

"No cleaning up," he said softly. He narrowed his eyes on her, trying to harden his facial features. "That's an order."

"I'm not one of your men that you can just order around." She poked him in the chest with her finger again.

He tightened his grip on her hand and let loose a low growl. Her hazel eyes darkened as she tipped her head back farther so she could look him in the eyes.

He closed the gap between them and pushed the proof of his arousal against her stomach. A gasp escaped her lips. She needed to know what she did to him. His cock begged for release from his jeans.

"You're right. I can't give them certain orders." He leaned down toward her.

She strained toward him, and he his crushed his mouth to hers. Her fingers gripped his shirt, and he pressed closer to her. Their lips molded together. He angled his head, and her lips parted, allowing his tongue to sweep into her mouth. He could taste the light wine still on her tongue.

His tongue plundered her mouth, and a moan released from her. Her soft lips moving across his lips had his cock straining against his jeans. He pulled back from her. She protested as he cupped her face in his large hands. He gently rubbed his thumbs over her cheeks, brushing her deep dimples. She gave him a small smile. He loved the caramel complexion of her skin. It was a direct contrast to the tan color of his. Everything about Sarena just made him want to go caveman on her.

Dragging her off to his bedroom and locking her away for him to have his way with her was quickly becoming his favorite fantasy.

Her tied up on his bed, naked, legs spread wide, waiting for him was an image that had a growl escaping his lips.

Soon.

"How about I give you an order I know you will follow," he murmured, laying another kiss on her swollen lips.

"What is that?" Her dazed eyes met his.

He smiled slightly and moved his thumb to her bottom lip. He couldn't stay away from her plump lips. They were perfect for kissing and wrapping themselves around his cock.

"Take your clothes off."

Sarena didn't move her gaze off Marcas as she reached for the bottom of her shirt. His order was said with such a commanding tone, that had she been one of his men, she would have scrambled to do what he ordered.

He was right.

This was an order he wouldn't be giving to his men.

This was just for her.

She pulled her shirt over her head. The chilled air met her skin, and her nipples drew up into painful beads, pushing against her bra. A quick intake of breath from Marcas, and her core clenched.

His eyes darkened as he moved his gaze down to take in her full breasts.

"All of them."

She tried to control her breathing and bit her lip. She slid her hands down to her jeans, unbuttoned them, and kicked off her heels, losing four inches of height. She felt so small and dainty near Marcas. He was a large man, and by the size of his bulge in his jeans, he was large everywhere. She shimmied out of her jeans, leaving herself in just her bra and panties.

"Are you taking anything off?" she asked, breathless. She took in his muscular frame, and her heart raced.

He shook his head.

"Off. All of it." He nodded to her chest; his gaze hadn't left her breasts.

She smiled, reaching behind and unsnapping the clasps of her lace bra. She dropped it to the floor before hooking her fingers underneath the waist of her panties. She was so thankful to Ronnie for talking her into getting her Brazilian earlier that week.

She kicked her panties off and stood before him with her hands on her hips, waiting on his approval. Her breasts ached to feel his hands on them as they swayed in the air.

"Good girl."

He moved as quick as lightning and scooped her up in his arms, and she gasped. He turned and sat her on the large marble island. Her ass met the coolness of the marble counter, and she shivered.

"Marcas," she whimpered. He spread her legs and stood between them. "You have too many clothes on."

"Don't worry about me," he growled, dipping his head into the crook of her neck.

He nipped her skin with his teeth before soothing it with his tongue, and she threw her head back.

She released a hiss, and he cupped her sensitive breasts in his hands and brought his lips to them. She moaned while he sucked one teat deep into his open, hot mouth. She buried her fingers in his short hair and held his head to her chest. He nuzzled and sucked on her soft mound then gave the other one attention.

"These breasts of yours are divine," he whispered against her nipple. His tongue blazed a hot trail along her skin as he moved toward her jawline.

She threw her fingers through his hair, anchoring his face in front of hers. Their lips merged together in a searing kiss. His large hands gripped her ass and pulled her toward the edge of the island. She wrapped her legs around his waist, holding him close to her. She slid her hands down to the edge of his shirt, but Marcas pulled back.

"Desert time," he murmured, pushing her back on the island.

The coldness of the countertop had goosebumps spreading along her skin, and she settled back. Her core clenched in anticipation of what was to come. He trailed his hands along her body, caressing her breasts and continued down her soft abdomen.

"Marcas." She groaned, the callused skin on his palms meeting the soft, supple skin of her inner thighs.

He pushed her legs apart, opening her to him. She bit her lip, loving the sensation of his fingers moving along her slit then dipping into her core.

"Just relax," he said.

Her body was strung tight. There was no way she would be able to relax. She was naked, spread-eagled on his kitchen island, and he wanted her to relax?

Not happening.

She was painfully aroused. Her breasts begged for attention, but at the moment, *his* attention was solely focused on her soaked pussy.

He released a growl, covering her pussy with his mouth. Her body arched off the counter as his tongue spread her labia and connected with her clitoris. Her eyes rolled into the back of her head when his tongue teased her clit. He sucked it deep within his mouth, and she thrust her pelvis toward his face.

He expertly flickered her small nub with his tongue, and her moans filled the air. She spread her legs wider to allow him to feast on her. Her breaths were coming faster, and she rocked her hips toward his face. She gripped his hair, riding his tongue, crying out, her body trembling.

Marcas ran his tongue along the entire length of her pussy, gathering her juices along the way toward her clit.

He knew how to bring her to the point where she

just wanted to scream for him to make her climax. His hands pushed her legs wide, and his tongue trailed along her anus then back to her core. The man was taking his sweet precious time while she wanted to reach her peak now.

His finger glided through the evidence of her desire and slid deep within her core.

"Marcas!" she cried out as he sucked on her swollen flesh.

He thrust a second finger deep inside her to join the first one, stretching her. Her entire body shook, her orgasm approaching.

She needed something to hold on to. She reached over her head and gripped the edge of the island, bracing herself for the impending orgasm.

A deep growl echoed around the room. She wasn't sure if it came from her or Marcas. He continued to thrust his fingers deep within her and latched on to her clit. The walls of her pussy tightened around his fingers as he pushed them deeper inside her. A scream tore from her lips, and the waves of her orgasm crashed into her.

7

Mac snatched Sarena from the island and hoisted her up flush to his body. Her legs immediately wrapped around his waist while he carried her from the kitchen. Her small hands forced his face to hers, then she slammed her mouth against his. Her tongue pushed its way into his mouth, boldly tangling with his.

He could feel and smell the evidence of her release coated on his face. Her taste was mind-blowing. He couldn't get enough of the sweet nectar that had flowed from her as she'd reached her orgasm. He loved the way her body was so responsive to his and knew that he wanted to explore what was between them all night.

There was no way she was going home soon.

He had plans for her that would take up most of their time together.

He gripped her naked ass tight in his hand, making his way into the living room without looking. His cock strained to be released. It demanded to plunge deep within her soaked core. Just imagining her pussy gripping his cock the way it had his fingers almost had him shooting off in his jeans.

He had the entire layout of his home memorized and could go through it blindfolded without bumping into one piece of furniture if need be. The way her lips moved across his face, her hips thrusting against his stomach almost frantically, he knew they weren't going to make it to the bedroom.

He needed to be balls deep in her tight little channel—now.

His oversized ottoman came into view. He moved toward it and tossed her down.

"Hey," she chuckled as she landed, but all laughter slowly erased from her face, and she sat frozen and watched as he pulled his shirt over his head and tossed it aside. "Sweet mother of God," she murmured, greedily taking in his naked chest.

Years spent in the service had been good for his physique.

Her gaze dropped to his hands to follow his motion of unbuttoning his jeans while he kicked his shoes off. Her eyes widened when he pushed his jeans down, exposing his large bulge underneath his boxer briefs, and his lips curved at the corners in a small smile.

"Boxer briefs. I knew it," she muttered, her attention not moving from his cock.

"Really?" He reached down and tipped her chin up so he could see her eyes. "So you've been thinking of the type of underwear I wear?"

"I've been thinking about more than just your underwear," she admitted, her wide eyes wider.

A growl rumbled low in his chest as he watched her hazel eyes darken.

"Is that so? What else has my little sex kitten been thinking about?"

His sex kitten? The way she'd whimpered and screamed on the counter with his tongue deep in her pussy had him thinking of a fully fledged tigress. The sting of nail marks on his shoulders burned, and he loved the battle wounds of making her reach a hard release.

"What your cock would taste like?"

He narrowed his eyes on her, and she shifted to sit on the edge of the ottoman. Her fingers slipped underneath the waist of his underwear and slowly pulled them down. His thick cock sprang free, and a gasp escaped her lips. Her wide eyes flew to his, and she gripped him in her small hand.

He released a curse. They maintained eye contact, and she licked the long length of him. His muscles grew tense. She slipped the head between her plump lips. If a gun was pressed his head, he wouldn't have been able to look away from the sight of Sarena swallowing him.

He knew his large cock was too much for her to take, but he could see she was trying her damnedest to fit in as much as she could. She pulled back, only leaving the tip, and he growled. His cock pulsed as she stroked him with her hand.

"Open your mouth wider," he ground out low in his throat.

He threaded his hand into her long thick hair, holding her in place, taking control and guiding his length between her lips.

She moaned, and he gently thrust into her mouth. Her eyes fluttered shut, and she ran her tongue along his length. His little tigress certainly knew how to suck a cock. His legs trembled from the sensations of her tongue and hot mouth taking him deep. It took everything he had to not pound away into her throat.

He bit back a curse knowing he wasn't going to last too long. Her small hand remained wrapped around his girth, sliding up and down the shaft along with her mouth. Her pace increased as she bobbed on him. Her eyes opened again and locked with his. His breaths were coming fast, a sign of the impending release.

He didn't want it to be over yet. He yanked his cock from her lips and silenced her protest.

"Not yet," he muttered, pushing her body back on the ottoman. He at first hadn't wanted the monstrous item in his living room but now he would be forever grateful the salesman had talked him into the purchase.

He covered her body with his, her legs immediately falling open to accommodate him. He braced the blunt tip of his cock at her soaked entrance and covered her lips with his.

Her mouth opened, allowing him to plunge his tongue inside at the same moment he thrust home. They cried out simultaneously, her tight walls gripping him. He paused to allow her to adjust to his invasion.

"Fuck, you're so tight," he muttered.

She whimpered. He growled, trying to get control of himself. Her slick walls encircled him, adjusting to the size of him. Nestled deep into her warm channel, he never wanted to leave.

She wrapped her arms and legs around him, then he pulled back and thrust again.

Nothing but the sounds of their fornication filled the air. Their eyes locked on one another, and he quickened his pace.

"Marcas," she gasped, bringing her hands to cup his jaw. She met him thrust for thrust, the proof of her arousal allowing his cock to slide easily into her. "Yes. God, yes!"

He crushed his lips to hers, his hips moving on instinct. Her bountiful breasts were crushed between them as she tried to get closer to him. His balls drew up close to his body, and he thrust deep. He gripped her hips tight, going on autopilot. Her slickness let him move freely inside her, driving him wild. They fit perfectly together.

She broke the kiss and she cried out, throwing her head back in ecstasy. Her walls clamped down on him, milking him into his own powerful orgasm. He roared his release as he poured himself into her.

Sarena thought things would be weird after their time in the kitchen or the living room.

Nope, not at all.

Marcas had refused to allow her to go home. His domineering nature attracted her to him. He had picked her up from the oversized ottoman and carried her up into his room where they'd spent the next few hours tangled up in the sheets of his bed. He didn't leave any part of her untouched. She could appreciate a man who wanted to make sure his partner was fully satisfied by morning. A slight soreness was developing in between her thighs, but it only brought a small smile to her lips as she lay tucked into his side.

His breaths were even while he slept, giving her time to study his silhouette in the dark. He was an alpha man all the way through. He had ensured she had reached her climax every single time before allowing himself the pleasure of release. She noticed how even in his sleep, his hand held on to her ass, keeping her close to him, her naked breasts pressed against his side, her head in the crook of his arm.

She didn't know what the morning would bring between the two of them. His rules of not dating left this pretty much up in the air. Was this a one-time hook-up? The chemistry between them was off the charts. It would be a waste, but she had known what she was getting into agreeing to this 'non-date'.

She gently caressed the light sprinkle of hair that littered his chest. She loved everything about his body. She couldn't find one flaw. The hard planes were cut with muscles that shouldn't even exist. Her core pulsed with just the thought of his thick cock. She held back a groan at the memories of taking it deep into her throat. The smoothness of his cock and the slight saltiness of his release still lingered on her tongue.

With the soft light flowing through the curtains on the windows, her motions on his chest woke his member. She smiled, making her hand go south. His abdomen quivered with her hand disappearing beneath the blanket. She wrapped it around his stiff length.

"I must not have done my job well enough," he murmured against her forehead. His voice was husky from sleep.

She could feel his eyes on her as she ran her hand along the mushroomed tip of his cock. His grip tightened on her ass cheek, and she pushed back the covers to allow his cock to spring free.

"I think you did your job too well," she said and playfully tightened her hand on his shaft. "I just can't stop thinking about this. I want it again."

"Well, then—"

The sound of an old ringtone slashed through the air, cutting him off. Marcas released a curse and reached over her toward the nightstand. He flicked the lamp on and grabbed his cell phone.

"Hold that thought," he muttered, swiping across the glass screen to answer. "What is it?" he growled into the phone.

She tucked the covers around her then sat up and leaned back against the plush pillows while he spoke to whoever was on the line.

Work.

She could tell because of his cold responses. Three in the morning, and she knew this wasn't a personal call. Something was going down, and SWAT was needed. He hung up and turned to her.

"You've got to go," she announced, looking at him.

He jerked his head in a nod. She glanced around the room and didn't see her clothes.

"Yeah. There's a situation over in Melrose Heights. A hostage situation."

"Go. I can let myself out." She moved to get out the bed, but he drew her back in. Surprised, she glanced up at him as he pulled her face close to his. He pressed a small kiss to her lips before easing back.

"You don't have to go now. Sleep," he ordered, standing from the bed.

He strode over to his dresser.

"I'm not one of your men, Sergeant," she murmured, sliding back down underneath the covers. She watched him dress, the pit of her stomach becoming queasy at the thought of him going off into a dangerous situation. The memory of his friend coming into the emergency room came to mind. She knew his job was dangerous and couldn't help but feel a small hint of fear for his safety.

He must have read her facial expression when he came out of his closet, decked out in black army fatigues.

"You certainly are not one of my men. I don't do

what I did with you with them." He chuckled, coming toward her.

She shifted her head back as he leaned over her, pressing a kiss to her lips. She opened her mouth, and he thoroughly kissed her, leaving her breathless when he moved away.

"Be careful," she murmured against his lips.

"Always."

8

"You're off," Declan acknowledged, coming to stand beside him as they took in the scene that was crawling with law enforcement.

The SWAT team was called in for a domestic disturbance in the area of Melrose Heights. A disgruntled man had barricaded himself in to one of the suburban homes with hostages. In these situations, SWAT was dispatched to ensure the livelihood of all parties involved. Mac and his team were able to make the entry into the home, clear it, and secure the hostages and the target. No causalities on this call.

He leaned back against the team's armored vehicle and looked to his longtime friend.

"What are you talking about?" he growled, his irritation growing at Declan's observance.

"Your mind wasn't on the mission," Declan replied, crossing his arms in front of his chest and glaring at Mac. "I know you. You moved through the motions, but you weren't the same 'pit bull' Mac who usually leads this team into a situation."

"Bullshit."

He didn't want to admit to his friend that he was correct. Since he'd left Sarena, his mind had been solely on her. He hadn't liked the look on her face when he'd come out of his closet. It was one he was all too familiar with when he left for deployment.

Fear.

That was the reason why he didn't do relationships.

But he couldn't get the memories or taste of her from his mind. Declan was right. It was dangerous to go into a situation and not be there mentally one hundred percent.

"Where were you when you got the call?"

"I was in my fucking bed," he snapped, pushing off the vehicle to face his friend. He didn't owe an explanation to anyone. He scowled at Declan, knowing his buddy knew him all too well.

"And who was in it with you?"

Mac turned away with a curse. He stood with his hands on his waist and looked out at the scene. The area was flooded with investigators and the local boys in blue. He watched one of the ambulances pull off, taking a hostage to the local hospital. He turned back to Declan knowing he couldn't lie to his friend.

"Sarena was with me," he admitted, pulling his helmet off his head. He ran a weary hand through his hair.

He met Declan's unwavering gaze. Declan was the first to look away with a curse.

"Listen, Mac. You know men like us aren't good with relationships," Declan began.

"We're not in a relationship. It was just fucking. Expelling some pent-up sexual frustration." Even to his ears, he didn't like the sound of his explanation.

As much as he didn't want to admit it, what he and Sarena had shared just hours before was more than 'just fucking'.

"I may have only met her once, but I can tell you that Sarena is definitely a woman who deserves a man's last name, Mac. Make sure she understands what she's getting into fucking around with you."

Declan moved to leave, but Mac growled, grabbing his friend's arm. Declan's eyes cut his, and they stood glaring at each other.

What could he say? He knew Declan spoke the truth. He just didn't want to admit it aloud.

"Everything all right over here?" Ashton said behind Mac.

He turned to find the rest of their team paused, watching them. Curiosity burned in all their eyes as they stared at Mac and Declan. Myles, Brodie, Ashton,

Zain, and Iker all stood poised as if ready to jump in to break up a fight between Declan and him.

Declan shook Mac's hand off. He stalked away around the armored truck then jumped into the back. Mac glanced back at the team and nodded.

"Yeah. We're good. Let's go. We need to go in for debriefing and fill out our reports," he snapped, waving them into the vehicle. He could see none of them believed him but he didn't have to explain himself to them or Declan. He hopped in behind them and shut the door.

Brodie tapped on the partition to let Iker know they were set and ready to go back.

Tension was thick in the vehicle as it pulled off. Mac knew his friend was right, but he didn't want to admit it. He knew Sarena understood. He had ensured she knew nothing would come of them being together.

He just didn't understand why it left a bad taste in his mouth.

"Hey, bestie!" Ronnie cried out, rushing in the door.

Ronnie Floyd and Sarena had been best friends since their sophomore year in college. They had met in nursing school and had to be lab partners. Ever since then, they had been glued at the hip to each other.

Ronnie was slightly taller than Sarena, with flawless mocha skin and long dark curls flowing down her back.

"Hey, Ronnie!" Sarena screamed and hugged her bestie. She laughed at the fact they were acting like they hadn't seen each other in days. No, they had just seen each other yesterday at work.

Sarena shut the door, and her friend moved into her home.

"Any updates?" Ronnie asked, throwing her purse on the couch and plopping down next to it. Her dark-brown eyes were wide as she waited to hear about Marcas.

It had been a few days since Sarena had woken up and put her clothes on to make the short walk of shame home after their non-date dinner. Due to him getting called out, they hadn't had to go through with the awkward 'morning after a one-night stand' routine.

"No." She shook her head and took a seat on the other end of the couch. She had confided in her friend about the night of passion she'd had with Marcas. "I'm really not expecting much."

"But if the chemistry is what you say it was, how can he just ignore it?" Ronnie sat back flabbergasted. She was a huge fan of romance and happy ever afters.

Sarena smiled at her gullible friend.

"This isn't one of those romance novels you read,

Ronnie." She shook her head at the look of hope on Ronnie's face. "Not everyone has a happy ever after."

"But you could! Have you called him?"

"Ronnie, he said he didn't do dating or relationships. I knew what I was going into when I went over to his place." She shrugged, thinking of her last few nights at home. She didn't know what he had done to her but she found herself wanting him even more. He filled her every thought.

She just couldn't get him out of her mind. Even now, her core pulsed with the memory of the feel of his cock stretching her walls when he'd thrust deep inside her. The feel of his hard body posed over her had chills sliding down her body. She was officially going through withdrawal. One night with Marcas MacArthur, and she was addicted. She craved another hit of his expertise tongue and thick cock.

She'd heard his motorcycle at all times of the night the last few days as he came and went. It took everything she had not to go to the window and try to catch a glimpse of him.

Even if she tried to be discreet, he would see her looking for him. She didn't want to appear desperate. If he wanted her, he would come for her.

"And you're just all right with this?" Ronnie's frustration was apparent on her face, and she stared at Sarena.

Was she okay with it? Not really, but she'd rather have one night with Marcas than nothing. She didn't regret their sole night together.

"I'm not going to be the desperate woman chasing him down. Believe me, I'd like nothing more than to walk over there and bang on the door and demand he fuck me again." She laughed, tucking a strand of her hair behind her ear.

She paused at the way Ronnie's eyes lit up.

"Oh no! There is no way in hell I can do that." She shook her head just as the sound of Marcas's motorcycle roared through the night, announcing he was home.

"Yes, you are! You are going to go over there in something sexy and you're going to get laid again tonight!" Ronnie shot off the couch and grabbed Sarena's hand. Her friend dragged her up the stairs and pushed her toward her bedroom.

"Ronnie, you are crazy. I can't just show up at the man's house and demand he take me, like one of the heroines in your books."

Ronnie pushed her into the room when Sarena tried to stall.

"If it works in the books, then it will work for you. How can he resist a hot babe like yourself?"

Her stomach fluttered just thinking of what could happen. But what if he only wanted her once? Doubt crept up in her mind, and she sat on the edge of her bed while Ronnie rummaged around in her drawers.

"But, Ronnie, what if the chemistry was just one-sided? What if I just imagined it? You're right. If it was there, wouldn't he have come for me again?" She bit her lip, her imagination running wild with the 'what ifs'. Self-doubt blossomed in her chest. What if their night together was the itch to his scratch and he was done with her?

"Don't you start doubting yourself, Sarena Rucker," Ronnie threatened and disappeared in Sarena's closet. "He should be grateful that you felt compelled to give him your cookie!"

Sarena snorted and crossed her arms in front of her chest. Felt compelled? She'd practically forced it down his throat.

Literally.

She watched her friend come out of her closet with a pair of fire-engine-red heels and lingerie in her hands. The glint in Ronnie's eyes made Sarena leery of her friend's plan.

"Um, where is the rest of the outfit?" she demanded to know.

Ronnie had lost her mind if she thought Sarena was going to walk over to his house in just lingerie and heels.

"This is it. You can throw your trench coat on over

it." Ronnie danced in place as she set the items down on the bed.

Sarena looked at the lingerie and recognized the piece. It was tiny, black, lace, and barely covered her body. She had bought it on a whim.

"You have officially lost your mind."

"Have I? Why buy these things if you aren't going to wear them?"

"I wear them," she muttered, picking up the lingerie and admiring it. It had been expensive, but she'd just had to have it. She hadn't been sure when she'd ever wear it, but she'd splurged and bought herself something sexy.

"When?" Ronnie cocked an eyebrow. She planted her hands on her hips, waiting for Sarena to reply. Her perfectly tweezed eyebrow was high on her forehead.

"Around the house when I need to feel sexy," Sarena mumbled, holding it to her chest. There was nothing wrong with a woman walking around her house in sexy lingerie to make her feel sexy.

"What am I going to do with you?" Ronnie exclaimed with a shake of her head. "No, this particular scrap of lace was meant for a man to peel off you with his teeth. Now go! Shower!"

"But, Ronnie—"

"Go!" Ronnie stomped her foot and pointed to Sarena's bathroom.

Sarena glanced down at the tiny scrap of lace and pondered for just a second.

Did she have big female balls to pull this off?

She thought of the night with Marcas and knew she had to have it again. Her dreams had been filled with nothing but memories of that night and even a few fantasies of what she prayed the future held. She looked up and met Ronnie's eyes.

"Okay, bitch. I'm going."

9

Mac stood beneath the steady flow of hot water. Steam filled the air as he braced his weight against the wall with his hand. Memories flooded his mind of his argument with Declan. His best friend had been right. In that short period of time, he'd let Sarena fill his thoughts and break his focus.

He'd tried his damnedest to get her out of his head. He'd tried to ignore the fact she lived next door. Close enough for him to walk over to her place and demand entrance, but he held himself back. He had to get the taste of her, or the sounds of her moans, from his mind.

Getting the call for the hostage situation had been a way for him to leave. It should have been an indicator of what a relationship with him would be like. He was always on call being a member of SWAT.

It was a demanding job that required many hours away from home. His unit not only served for the local police department but for the Feds as well. The last two days had been spent going through tactical training. To be the best, he and his team had to rack up countless hours of training to ensure they were top notch.

The days consisted of going through drills to practice and perfect their entry into buildings, sweeps, and takedowns. His body ached from the hand-to-hand combat drills. Declan, as usual, was his partner and hadn't taken it easy on him. They were evenly matched in size and strength. They had gone at each other with a ferociousness that allowed them to pound out their frustrations. By the end of training, they were good and back to old pals. His team had ended the session with time at the shooting range.

As usual, Myles had showed them all up with his precision shooting. Mac was a spot-on shooter, but Myles had the eyes of cat and could hit targets at over five hundred yards.

The water pounded on his head as he stepped underneath the warm spray. Visions of Sarena's caramel skin came to mind. He released a curse and tried to push it away, but his mind was playing tricks on him.

He closed his eyes, and the sight of her spread out on his bed woke the hunger for her again. His cock thickened with the thought of his tongue flicking her pink pearl that lay hidden in between her brown folds.

He released a growl as he connected his hand with his aching member. He stroked himself to the memory of his cock disappearing between her plump lips with her eyes locked on him. Her hot little mouth knew how to work him up into a frenzy that no woman had been able to do before.

He released a grunt and moved his hand faster. He gripped himself tight, closing his eyes, imagining all the ways he would love to take her but hadn't got the chance to.

The memory of her eyes widening when he had proclaimed that he would have her everywhere came to mind. He knew she had been in a state of frustration when he'd left her on the porch that time. He'd read her face easily. She wanted him.

He'd had her, but it wasn't enough. By the evidence of how hard his cock currently was for her, there was no way in hell he was done with her.

He pumped his fist faster, imagining his cock sliding into her tight channel, her legs wrapping around him as she threw her head back in ecstasy. His balls tightened, hot spurts of release shooting out. His eyes tightened, too, and he pumped a few more times, expelling his release. He paused, gripping his semi-hard length, and the realization hit him square in the chest.

Sarena belonged to him, in his bed, in his arms, and sliding down on his cock.

Damn the rules.

He leaned back and let the water rush over him. Determined, he quickly washed his body. Going against everything he had convinced himself of over the years, he would go to her. She was a smart woman and would understand what it would mean to be with a cop. They would take it one day at a time. No need to rush into anything.

He rinsed, shut the water off, then stepped out of the shower and grabbed his towel. Wrapping it around his waist, he stalked into his bedroom, trying to think of all the things he could say to Sarena to explain why he hadn't called or had any contact with her. He grabbed a pair of sweats and threw them on. The sound of his doorbell floated through the air, and he finished toweling off his chest and ran it over his hair to dry it a little.

"Who the hell is that?" he muttered, glancing at the bedside clock.

It was a little after nine at night, and he wasn't expecting anyone. He moved to his nightstand and pulled his Glock from the drawer, flipping off the safety and creeping to the top of his stairs. His bare feet flew down the steps as he made his way toward the front of his house.

He arrived at the door and pulled it open without looking. Whoever it was would be greeted by the nozzle of his Glock. Mac froze in place at the sight that met him.

"Well, is that how you normally greet your neighbor?" Sarena breathed, her gaze dropping down to the weapon in his grip. She propped her hand on the edge of the doorframe and settled the other on her hip.

He slowly took her in. She was the epitome of sexiness. His tongue was stuck to the roof of his mouth as his eyes met hers.

He trailed his gaze down over her. Her thick hair fell around her shoulders in waves. She had a beige trench coat on that stopped mid-thigh. Her silky brown legs went on for miles and were put on display by her red high heels.

"Sarena," he said, clearing his throat, his voice finally able to work. He shook his head to erase all the erotic images that were coming to mind.

"Are you going to invite me in, Marcas?"

Something about the way she said his name always had his heart skipping a beat. He usually went by Mac, never Marcas, but it felt right coming from her. She'd be the only person he'd allow call him by his first name besides his mother.

His eyes met hers again, and he pushed the door open and granted her entrance. She brushed past him with a small smile on her face. He shut the door behind her and turned to her. He leaned back against the door, unsure why she was there. He hadn't called her, and here she was, standing in his entryway, dripping sex appeal.

"Are you going to hold on to the gun? It makes this a little awkward if you feel you need to be armed." She cocked her eyebrow at him, nodding to the weapon in his hand.

He flipped the safety back on and pushed off the door.

"I usually keep it secured in my bedroom," he murmured and moved past her toward the living room. He walked over to the entertainment center and pulled open one of the draws. The sound of her heels on his hardwood floors echoed behind him. He placed the gun in the drawer for now, making a mental note to come back later to put it where it belonged. "Why are you here?

He turned around, and the wind left his lungs as if he had been hit in the chest with a two by four.

Sarena held back the chuckle at the look on Marcas's face. She cocked her hip and rested her hands on them while he took her in. She had removed her jacket once he'd gone into the living room.

Now here she stood in her little lace lingerie that molded to her thick curves and did nothing to hide anything. Her core clenched at the hunger that burned from his irises as he eyed her up and down.

Ronnie had been right. This outfit was much better suited to show off in front of a man. One who would peel it off of her.

She grinned and slowly turned around so he could see the full outfit. The lingerie was designed for a woman with an ample backside, and she had plenty. The back of the bottoms were a thong, leaving both plump ass cheeks of hers on display. She pulled her long hair over her shoulder so he could see the full outfit.

She stared over at Marcas with an innocent look on her face. His gaze was locked on her ass, and she knew she had him. No man could fight a woman in a sexy outfit that highlighted everything he loved about the female anatomy, and Marcas MacArthur was an ass and breast man.

"Like what you see, Marcas?" she murmured, turning back to face him. She put a little sway in her hips as she made her way over to him.

Now it was her turn to lay down the rules.

After her pep talk from Ronnie, she was confident in her sex appeal and knew if she wanted Marcas, she'd just have to go after him and make him see things her way. He didn't get to just decide for her. He just didn't know what he wanted and didn't realize that what they'd started the other night was nowhere near finished.

"Fuck, Sarena." He ran his hand through his hair when she stopped in front of him.

She cocked her head back so she could gaze into his eyes.

"That's what we are going to do, Marcas." She smiled at the sight of his nostrils flaring. She had him in the palm of her hand. No matter how much he tried to fight what was between them, she'd win him over. They could work out the details of their 'relationship' later. Now, she just needed him between her legs.

She placed her finger over his lips as he opened his mouth to speak.

"Shh..." She pressed her body to his. His cock pushed against her through his cotton sweats, and it took all she had to stay focused and not drop to her knees in front of him. "Now see here, Sergeant Marcas MacArthur. It wasn't that long ago that you marched over to my yard and told me that we were going to fuck. Now it's my turn."

He moved to speak again, and she rested her finger

on his lips and shushed him once more. He wasn't about to kill her thunder, she was on a roll.

"I'm not done. We are going to fuck. Many times. And we are going to date. I don't care what you've done in the past, I'm the present, and if you play your cards right, I'll be your future. I want you to peel this contraption off me, fuck me hard all night, and then tomorrow, we'll discuss our relationship. Do you follow me, Sergeant?"

Her breaths were coming fast, and she waited for an answer. He cocked his eyebrow and glanced down at her finger. She removed it to allow him to talk.

"Do I have permission to speak, ma'am?"

A dangerous glint appeared in his eyes, and her core clenched. His hand slid up to the back of her neck and held her head in place.

"Yes, Sergeant," she breathed, watching his head move close to her. "You have permission."

"Good. I'm a fucking idiot," he muttered then swooped his mouth down onto hers.

The kiss was hot, open, and wet. She celebrated her victory by wrapping her arms around his neck. His hands instantly cupped her bare ass, crushing his hard cock to her stomach.

She released a moan as his tongue thrust its way inside her mouth. Marcas grabbed her and lifted her.

She instantly wrapped her legs around his waist and held on for dear life when he moved toward the stairs.

She'd have to call and thank her friend tomorrow. Hopefully, she'd have some form of her voice left. Tonight, she planned for there to be plenty of screaming.

10

Marcas burst through the door of his bedroom. She could still smell the lingering scent from his soap in the air and on him. She groaned as his hand gripped her ass cheek. They had yet to break their kiss. She moved her lips to his scruff-lined jaw. His shadow of a beard drove her crazy. Just the memory of the scruff scraping against the soft skin of her thighs had her core clenching.

He strode across the bedroom with her in his arms. His strength amazed her since she was a thick woman. He stood near the bed and allowed her to slide down his body. She groaned, her body coming into contact with every hard part of his muscular frame. His warm chest called for her lips. She trailed kisses along his chest, standing on her own two feet.

He whipped her around and pulled her back to his chest. His hand crept up to her neck and held her in place, and he nuzzled the crook of her neck.

"Sarena, forgive me." he murmured. "I'll explain later, okay?

"You don't have to explain anything," she whispered, his grip on her throat tightening.

He moved her head to the side to allow his lips to have the freedom to brush along her neck.

"I do, but right now I have orders to follow."

She could feel his lips curve up in a smile.

"That you do, Sergeant," she said.

He pushed her onto her stomach on the edge of the bed, putting her ass on display for him, and she let loose a gasp. She looked over her shoulder and found his eyes locked on her ass as he massaged her plump globes.

Her pussy grew slick with need at the hunger that was apparent on his face. A growl released from him, and he landed a sound smack to her right ass cheek. Her body jerked, and the sting that followed had her core clenching. She bit her lip, and he rubbed the area with his hand, soothing the skin.

"If you really like this thing, you better tell me how to get you out of it, or I'm ripping it off," he warned.

She chuckled, knowing she'd spent too much money on it, and with his reaction to it, she would keep it and definitely wear it again. She quickly disrobed, but he wouldn't allow her to move from her position.

"Stay just how you are," he whispered in her ear, bending over her.

His lips burned a trail along her shoulder blades and down the curve of her back. He spread her legs wide, making his way to her ass. He nipped the cheeks of her ass, and she giggled.

Her smile disappeared when he spread her cheeks and trailed his tongue around her forbidden hole. She bit down on the comforter and cried out. He continued his exploration of her ass with his tongue and teeth. Her nipples, hard as diamonds, pressed against the bed, and she angled herself to ensure he could reach every facet of her that he wanted. His tongue continued farther down, dipping into her dripping pussy.

She dug her nails into the bed as he licked her clean and trailed her moisture back up to her puckered entrance.

"Marcas," she cried out, her body shaking from his assault.

He continued his actions, drawing her wetness to her dark hole.

She grew excited, knowing he was preparing her for him. She glanced over her shoulder to see him stand and untie his pants. Their eyes locked, his pants sliding to the floor, allowing his cock to spring free. His magnificent member stood erect from his body. She licked her lips at the sight of his thick cock that she knew was about to bring her much pleasure.

"Turn back around," he ordered, landing another smack to her ass cheek.

She gasped, moisture seeping from between her folds from the sting left by his hand. She was aroused beyond belief. She turned her head away and dug her fingers into the comforter again.

The blunt tip of his cock pushed on her labia. He rubbed himself against her pussy, gathering her lubrication on the head of his cock. He slowly thrust his thick member inside her slick pussy. Her juices coated him, allowing him to slide deep within her. They both released a groan, her walls gripping him tight. He pulled back and this time drove in deeper, hitting the entrance to her womb with his cock tip. She rocked her hips to meet each of his thrusts. His hands came around her and gripped her breasts, holding her in place, his motions increasing. Each thrust felt deeper, and the angle of her body allowed him to go deep.

So deep.

She cried out as she jutted her hips back toward him, needing him. His cock stretched her to the point of a fullness she never wanted to go away.

He withdrew from her, and she cried out. The sounds of their labored breathing filled the air.

"Sarena," he murmured her name, his fingers replacing his cock.

With her face buried in the covers, her response was muffled. Her attention was on the sensation of his fingers dipping within her and drawing her slickness toward her dark hole.

"Marcas," she moaned, releasing the blanket from her mouth.

His cock brushed against her pussy, this time sliding right home. He held still, and she was tempted to turn and curse him to get him to move again.

"I want my cock here," he ground out, pushing a single finger into her tight hole. She cried out from the feel of her forbidden entrance being stretched while his cock stayed buried in her pussy. "Can I take you here?"

His finger lodged as far as it would go, and he twisted it around. It was a feeling she had yet to experience before. No other lover had been worthy enough to get that kind of action with her.

With Marcas, she was willing to try anything. She glanced over her shoulder and met his waiting eyes. Her heart raced, and her breaths were coming fast as she gazed into his intense eyes.

Yes, he could have her any way he wanted her.

"God, yes. Marcas. Please."

He withdrew his finger from her, and she turned

her head back and bit her lip while she waited. She was close to climaxing. Her body was strung tight from the sensations he wrung out of her.

The blunt tip of his cock pressed against her dark hole. She held her breath, and he eased forward, slowly introducing inch by inch of him into her. His large girth fit snug inside her, giving her a new fullness she'd never experienced before.

She loved it. Every part of it.

"Oh God," she cried, her dark entrance stretching farther than it had ever been. The slight burn felt so good, she closed her eyes and gripped the covers tight in her fist, Mac settled balls deep in her.

"Are you all right?" he asked, covering her back with his body.

She nodded, unable to answer. She knew he was taking it slow and remaining still to give her a moment to adjust to the invasion. His hands came up around her and gripped her breasts again, as if to anchor himself to her. He pulled back and thrust again, this time hard, and she cried out in ecstasy.

"Yes!"

He repeated his motion over and over. She cried out again, loving the feel of him taking her in the ass. She thrust back, meeting him as he gripped her tight to him.

He quickened his thrusts, and she chanted his

name over and over. Marcas MacArthur was consuming her. She would get what she asked for. She'd practically ordered him to fuck her hard, and that was exactly what he was doing.

His hand slid down her abdomen and dove between her folds, finding her swollen clit. He drew her slickness to her tiny bundle of nerves and strummed her sensitive flesh. That was all she needed to tip her over.

"Marcas!" she screamed, her orgasm slamming into her.

He released a grunt. Her body shook with the waves of her release flooding her. He roared behind her and emptied himself into her.

Mac pulled Sarena close to him as he shifted in the bed. Her delicious nakedness was pressed to his side, and he didn't want it any other way. He opened his eyes and glanced down at her, finding a small smile on her lips. She snuggled closer to him, and he adjusted the blanket over them to ensure she was comfortable. He leaned back against the pillows, thinking of the way she had strode in the house and basically laid down the law.

He chuckled with the thought of her feistiness. His

cock jumped with the memory of her standing in her barely there lingerie, and he knew he couldn't wake her. They'd made love for hours, and she had just gone to sleep about fifty minutes ago.

He'd let her rest for now, but in the morning, he couldn't promise he'd be able to keep his hands, tongue, or cock away from her.

His eyes closed but flew back open at the sound of the ringing of a phone. He groaned, thinking it couldn't be a worse time to receive a call. He glanced over at the clock on his nightstand and found it to be a little after four in the morning. He reached over and grabbed his phone, but his was silent.

Her phone was ringing.

"Sarena," he murmured, rubbing his hand along her back and settling it on her ass. What an ass it was. He grinned at everything he'd done to her perfectly plump rear. He felt the shiver that passed through her body. "Baby. Wake up. Your phone is ringing."

Her eyes opened and were clouded with sleep. He was learning fast that she was a hard sleeper. He shook his head. Her confused eyes turned to him.

"Sarena. Your phone."

"At this time? Oh God!"

She scrambled to break free from the blankets and turned on her side to grab her phone. She swiped the screen, but he caught the words 'blocked' on the screen before she placed it to her ear. "Hello."

He knew it was none of his business who was calling and he couldn't help but notice a slight twinge of an emotion he'd never experienced before rear its head in his chest.

Was this jealousy?

He caught the sound of a deep voice coming through the phone, and his curiosity was piqued.

"Harden?" she exclaimed, sitting up. A wide grin spread across her face as she relaxed against the pillows.

Her infamous brother.

He laid back, too, and tossed his arm across his face to give her some privacy. After her announcement that she did have a sibling, Mac had gone back to the service he'd employed to run checks and informed them of their mishap. This was the first mistake he'd been aware of them making and demanded they find out about Harden Rucker. But of course, being a civilian company, they weren't privileged to the more sensitive information of members of the armed forces that didn't want to be found. So he'd had to call in a favor with his contacts he still had with the Navy to find out about Sarena's brother and should be hearing from them any day.

"I'm good. I miss you," she said, shifting on the pillows.

He tried to act like he wasn't listening to her side of the conversation but he couldn't help but be all ears.

"Have you called Mom and Dad yet to check in?"

Why would Harden erase himself from anything that would pull up for family? Something like this meant her brother was deep and didn't want any traces of family tied to him.

"What do you mean 'where am I'?" she asked.

His muscles tensed, he waited for her to answer.

"Oh, you called my house? Well, no, I'm not home…I know what time it is here. I can tell time just fine."

He could hear the deep voice growing louder, and Mac turned over so he could openly look at her. Her eyes met his as he tugged the blanket down from her breasts. It should be against the law to cover up something as magnificent as them. Her whole damn body should never be clothed. He had made sure he'd taken the time to taste every single part of her body, from her lips on down to her tiny toes.

He figured he'd have fun while she was on the phone with her brother and tweaked a nipple.

"It's none of your business, big brother," she scoffed and rolled her eyes, holding the phone away from her ear.

Harden Rucker wanted to know where his sister was? Mac would help him figure out quick and make him regret calling Sarena at this time of night.

Mac knew that the Navy SEAL was probably in some undisclosed country on a later time zone, trying to touch base with family. Mac had plenty of memories of apologizing for waking his parents when he'd call to check in.

"Well, if you must know, I'm over at my neighbor's house," she breathed.

He licked her perky nipple. Her eyes grew wide, and she tried to push him away.

"Are you crazy?" she mouthed to him, batting him away again.

Her eyes widened even farther as he reached for her again. He chuckled, loving this game. He moved closer to her but stopped when her body stiffened.

"Marcas MacArthur did what?" she shrieked and scooted over to put distance between them.

Her eyes narrowed on him. He swore under his breath, realizing Harden must have found out he was enquiring about him.

"I'm here with him now," she said.

"Sarena, I can explain," he murmured, but she cut him off with a finger in the air.

"Of course I'm safe, Harden," she assured.

She glared at him, eyes still narrowed. He met her

gaze, not ashamed at looking into her or her brother. As a SEAL, her brother would understand.

"So you ran a check on him, too, huh? Navy SEAL. Uh-huh. I know. I'm certain. Okay. I love you, too. Be safe and call me as soon as you can."

Mac stared into her hazel eyes and knew he may have some groveling to do. This was unfamiliar territory for him, and he quickly wondered if it was going to be worth it. She tossed the phone to the nightstand and turned to him. The sight of her brown areolas captivated him, and he knew the answer.

She was worth it.

11

Sarena looked up from her computer and found Ronnie standing in the doorway of her office. For the last few hours she had been working on auditing patient's charts. It was one of the parts of the job she detested, but her boss assured her it was not something they could stop.

She just couldn't believe that Marcas had run a background check on her—yet she could. What had left her speechless was that he'd looked into her brother, and her brother, in turn, had checked him out. It was just too much to handle. It was like two alpha males sizing each other up without even meeting. She'd been ecstatic to hear from her brother with him being deployed, but for him to fall into this game with Marcas just left her shaking her head.

"Hey, Ronnie, what's up?" She motioned her friend into her office and let loose a sigh as she ran a hand through her hair.

"Just checking in on you," she replied, plopping down in the chair in front of Sarena's desk. "So what is going on with you and the neighbor? One minute I'm sending you off over to his house like a hooker going to be with her first john, and the next, I don't hear from you."

"Ronnie!" Sarena rolled her eyes.

"Okay, maybe not a hooker. But you were smoking hot," Ronnie muttered, shrugging. "So what gives? I send you over there and I was expecting a full report the next morning—excuse me—afternoon."

Sarena thought of her second night with Marcas. It had begun as a wonderful evening of insane chemistry and setting fire to the sheets of Marcas's bed. A smile appeared on her lips with the thoughts of the things they'd done. She'd done things with Marcas she'd never even desired until now. It had been a magical night until Harden interrupted their time together.

She truly loved her brother. She did, but his timing couldn't have been worse.

"Well, without giving away all the sexy details, let's just say the outfit worked," she began, a grin spreading across her face.

Ronnie danced in her chair, her squeal of delight cutting Sarena off. "I knew it! So, did he peel it off with his teeth?" Her friend sat forward with wide eyes, waiting for Sarena to respond.

"I'm not going to divulge the details of my wicked night with the SWAT sergeant." She laughed, teasing. "At least, not here at work, my friend."

"Well, at least tell me he has a buddy." Ronnie pouted, crossing her arms in front of her chest.

"Well, actually, he does," she murmured, thinking of Declan, the man she'd had the pleasure of meeting after he had been shot.

"And you're just now saying something?" A playful, hurt expression appeared on Ronnie's face, and Sarena chuckled.

"He's pretty hot, too, in an intense, macho-alpha kind of way," Sarena teased again.

"I don't think our friendship is as tight as it used to be." Ronnie shook a finger at Sarena, who giggled even more. "Nope. We need to reevaluate this relationship."

"When the opportunity comes up, I will introduce you to Declan," she promised, wiping her tears from her face. Her promise seemed to calm Ronnie down. "I wouldn't want you to break up with me after all these years."

"I'm going to hold you to it, too, dammit." Ronnie smiled, flipping her hair over her shoulder. "Best friend code. Ensure your bestie meets hot guy's hot friend."

"Are you on your lunch?" She changed the subject. She was starting to feel slight hunger pains and glanced down at her watch. It was getting late, and she figured she should grab a bite to eat.

"Nope. I was going to go get coffee and figured I'd walk up here and see if you wanted to go down to the coffee shop with me."

"That sounds wonderful," she breathed, sitting back from her desk. She could use a little caffeinated boost to get through the rest of her shift. She'd grab something to eat while she grabbed coffee. "Let's go now, before change of shift. I'm short a nurse and will have to pick up an assignment for the last four hours."

They walked out of her office. She called out to one of her nurses and let her know she was running down for coffee.

"Hey, Sarena! Someone's out in the front waiting room asking for you," Liza hollered from the front of the department.

Sarena glanced over at the doors that led to the waiting area of emergency.

"Well, who the hell could that be?" she muttered. "Give me a second, Ronnie."

"Go ahead. I'll be over at the nurses' station." Ronnie waved to one of the nurses as she made her way over there.

Sarena headed toward the double doors that Liza had just disappeared through. Liza was one of the receptionists who worked the front desk where patients checked in on arrival to the hospital.

She pushed through the double doors and walked through the short maze that led to the waiting area. Liza was seated at her desk behind the glass window, typing on her computer.

"Did they say what they want?" Sarena asked, coming to stand next to Liza. It was probably a disgruntled patient or family member needing to speak to the manager on duty.

Liza let loose a deep sigh and braced her head on her hand as she pointed out into the waiting room.

"It's the sexy cop over there," she murmured. "He could lock me up any day."

Sarena's gaze flew to the corner of the empty waiting room where a tall, muscular figure stood staring out the window.

Marcas.

He was decked out in his black tactical uniform. He was everything that any woman who fantasized about a sexy police officer would be.

Utility belt with handcuffs.

Gun in the holster.

She let loose a sigh and agreed with Liza.

He could lock her up anytime he wanted.

He turned as if feeling eyes on him and met her

gaze through the safety glass of the reception window. Her mouth grew dry at his heated look.

"Man, what I wouldn't do to have his attention." Liza chuckled, clearly observing the sparks flying between Sarena and Marcas.

Ignoring the comment, she headed through the receptionist area and toward the doors to the waiting room.

What was he doing here?

Once she had left his house after their magical night, she hadn't seen him. She had worked every day since, and the absence of his bike let her know he had barely been home as well.

She pushed through the doors to the waiting room and paused, trying to catch her breath as all the memories from the other night rushed forward.

Mac waited for Sarena to appear. He didn't know why he'd just showed up at the hospital on a whim but he knew he had to see her. He'd had some explaining to do once she was off the phone with her brother.

Mac had never been one to have to explain himself to a woman, but this time he'd found himself explaining his actions before he'd even realized the words were flowing from his mouth.

"You ran a background check on me, like I'm some criminal?" she asked, pulling the covers back over her breasts.

He immediately saw the apprehension enter her eyes as she stared at him.

"No. I did it before meeting you. I like knowing who is moving into the neighborhood."

"So instead of doing like any other normal neighbor would do and come meet me, you instead invaded my privacy and researched me?"

She slowly stood from the bed, and he knew this was going south.

Fast.

"Sarena." He shifted to her side of the bed, placed his feet on the floor, and paused when she backed away from him. He released a curse and stood. *"Really, I didn't mean anything by it."*

"But why would you be looking into my brother?"

Her hand trembled as she pushed her hair back away from her face.

"Just because I thought it was odd that when I read your report, it didn't give any mention of a sibling, and then you admitted to having a brother."

"What do you mean it didn't mention my brother?"

"He was not listed as your brother. It had you listed as an only child."

"But how can that be?"

Her eyes were wide. He slowly made his way to her and breathed a sigh of relief when she allowed him to bring her to him. His heart raced, and he tried to will it to slow down.

Was this fear?

Fear of losing Sarena?

He gazed down into her hazel eyes and reached up to cup her face in his hand. Fear radiated from her eyes. The urge to erase all worry and doubt from her grew in his chest.

"I'm sure there is a reason. I'm not sure what your brother is into, but something or someone triggered that I was looking into him. He must not want to be found," he murmured.

Unable to resist her kiss-swollen lips, he placed a small peck on them.

"I'm sure he's being the big, bad SEAL and is doing something dangerous that he knows will worry me and my mother."

He wasn't sure who she was trying to convince, her or him. He tightened his grip on her to reassure her.

"I've been where he's at and I'm sure it's for your safety." He pushed her hair behind her ear.

Her body softened against his as he pulled her tighter to him. He slid the sheet from in between them, leaving them naked, nestled close to each other. His cock took notice of her soft curves pressed to it and immediately stiffened.

"You know I'm still going to be mad at you." *She cocked an eyebrow at him, reaching up and entwining her fingers behind his neck.*

"I think I can handle it," he said then covered her mouth with his.

"Hey." Sarena's small voice brought him out of his memories. A shy smile lingered on her lips as she looked at him.

"Hey," he said, suddenly unsure why he was really there. His face grew warm at his uncertainty.

What. The. Fuck.

Mac never got embarrassed or was unsure when it came to females.

Her dimples deepened with her widening smile. He cursed under his breath, and she giggled at his nervousness.

Here he was, Sergeant Marcas MacArthur, former Navy SEAL, current SWAT officer, who had faced the worst enemies that anyone could imagine, standing here literally tongue-tied.

"Look, I'll admit I don't know why I'm here." He ran a hand through his hair.

She moved to stand directly in front of him, and he ached to pull her flush to his body, but there were several things that kept him from doing so.

The large erection pressing against his cargo pants. No need to cause him any more discomfort.

He was in full uniform, since he was on his way in to the station for his shift.

And not to mention the crowd of nurses who were gathering behind the glass window, making no excuses for staring at them.

"That's okay. Let me guess, you were in the neighborhood?" She cocked her sexy eyebrow up at him, seemingly unaware her friends were watching and eavesdropping on their entire conversation.

His lips jerked into a rare smile.

"Yeah, something like that?" He folded his arms across his chest. He tried to will his cock to settle down, but it had a mind of its own. "I'm on my way to work and I get off in the morning. How about tomorrow night we go out? Dinner and a movie?"

Her eyebrows shot up high, and he held back a groan and knew instantly she was about to bust his balls. She sidled up closer to him, leaving only a hair's-breadth of distance between them.

"But, Sergeant, I remember you announcing that you didn't date." Her perfect teeth were showing with her wide grin as she brought up the day on her porch. "I remember you mentioned that you usually don't—"

He held up his hand to stop her. He rolled his eyes,

and she burst out laughing. She fell into his body, hers racked with laughter.

"Okay, you got me," he muttered, grasping her hip with his hand.

She leaned into him, her laughter fading. He knew she was totally oblivious of the crowd hanging on to their every word and movement. He didn't care that they were watching. He could tell by their shit-eating grins they were excited and happy for Sarena.

Might as well give them a show, he thought to himself.

"I do?" she murmured, staring up into his eyes.

"You were very persuasive with your orders. So tomorrow, you and I are going to go on an old-fashioned date. I'll pick you up at seven sharp," he announced.

He gripped her chin with his free hand and lowered his mouth to hers. Her plump lips welcomed his in a soft, sweet kiss. He desired a deeper one but had to remember he was in her place of employment.

Muffled cheers and whistles echoed through the air, and Sarena jumped back from him as if she were a teenager getting caught necking by her parents. She glanced over her shoulder at the receptionist window and laughed, covering her face. He held her in place, not ashamed to be witnessed kissing the sexiest nurse alive. He shook his head and threw the women a wink, and they hooted and hollered even more.

She groaned, leaning her head against his chest in embarrassment.

"I expect a great action-packed movie, popcorn, and then an amazing dinner," she said, wrapping her arms around his waist.

The catcalls and cheers continued, and she smiled.

"You'll get all that and dessert," he whispered into her ear. He could feel the shiver pass through her body. The darkening of her eyes let him know she'd got his message loud and clear.

12

Sarena breathed deeply, pushing through the last of her run. She turned the corner of the street that led to her house. Relief filled her as her place came into sight. It had been a few days since her last run, and she needed to expel some energy.

His sudden appearance at her job last night had left her hot and bothered. She could barely concentrate for the rest of her shift. Lucky enough, one of her nurses asked to stay the last four hours to pull a double. Sarena would have been all over the place had she needed to take an assignment. The emergency room picked up after Marcas had left, leaving her last few hours to fly by.

Finally, she reached the sidewalk in front of her home and eased her jog to a walk to try to lower her heart rate. The sound of a car slowing filled the air. She ignored it and walked up her driveway with her hands on her hips. She tried to breathe in deeply to calm her body down, but it currently wasn't working. Those few days without running was catching up with her.

The sound of the car turning into her driveway grabbed her attention. She turned to see a black sedan coming to a halt a few feet from her.

Sarena squinted but was unable to see who was inside. She wasn't expecting any company, and the vehicle was unfamiliar.

The driver rolled down his window as she walked toward the car. A man in his mid-thirties to early forties smiled at her from the driver's seat.

"Morning," he called out.

"Good morning. Can I help you?" Unease filled her chest, and she stopped a few steps before the car.

"Yes, does Sheila Caspin live here? I seem to have gotten turned around." He chuckled, his arm hanging out of the window.

His demeanor seemed friendly, but she couldn't shake the uneasy feeling he gave her. His mouth was stretched into a smile, but something was off about him.

The smile doesn't reach his eyes.

"I'm sorry. You have the wrong house," she announced, the feeling of unease growing stronger when his gaze perused down her body.

Creep.

"Is this 22553 Hilton East?" he asked, tearing his gaze away from her to look down at a piece of paper.

"No, Hilton is a few streets that way." She pointed in the direction he needed to go. "At the stop sign, make a right and drive down about half a mile and then you'll see it on the right."

"Thanks." His smile widened at her.

Relief filled her at the sound of another vehicle coming down the road. She flicked her eyes in that direction. Marcas flew down the street in his oversized truck. He slowed and pulled into his driveway then drew to a halt at the edge of his walkway. Their eyes met before his attention turned to the man in the vehicle.

"Good luck finding your friend," she said, turning back to the stranger.

She backed away from the car to try to give him the hint it was time to leave. The sound of Marcas's door slamming shut echoed through the air.

"I'm Silas, by the way." He laughed. "I know this may seem odd, but what's your name—"

"Taken," a deep baritone voice interrupted.

She smiled, feeling Marcas arrive behind her. His possessive arm sneaked its way around her waist and pulled her back against him. She looked over her shoulder and found his glare directed at Silas.

Her heart fluttered at the feel of him behind her. Her core clenched at his dominant nature.

"Wow, um...my bad." Silas held up his hands in defeat with shock appearing on his face. He eyed Marcas briefly before his focus turned back to Sarena. His smile was forced, and he nodded. "Beautiful woman, man. Couldn't help but try."

Marcas moved to her side and didn't reply but kept his eyes trained on the man as he threw his car in reverse. She turned and looked at him. His muscles were drawn tight while he watched the car leave her driveway and go off in the direction she had instructed him to.

"He had the wrong address," she murmured, running her hand along his chest.

He grunted a response but had yet to take his attention off the car as it disappeared from their street.

"It's okay," she said.

"It's not," he muttered, turning back to her.

She smiled, and his eyes darkened as he gazed into her eyes. She knew she was a sweaty mess from her run. Her sports bra and performance shorts were all soaked with perspiration. She didn't even want to know what her face and hair looked like.

"I didn't like the way he was staring at you."

"I can tell." She laughed, loving his possessiveness. "I was expecting you to growl and go all 'my woman'."

"Something like that. I already told you that your jogging outfits drive me crazy. Any man with a pulse would ogle you."

"Well, thank goodness I'm only interested in one man ogling me." She batted her eyes up at him. It was the truth. In the few short months she had lived next to him, he was the only one she had been trying to catch. Now she literally had him in her grasp, she couldn't care less about any other man.

"Damn right I'm ogling." He tried to pull her closer, but she pushed off away from him.

"I'm too sweaty." She laughed again, shaking her head. She needed to take a shower. There was no telling how bad she reeked.

"You think I care about sweat?" he growled, pulling her flush against him.

"You know Janet is probably glued to her window, watching us." She laughed once more, thinking of their nosey neighbor. For all the information that woman had on the people, Sarena was surprised their neighbor was able to sleep.

"Let her look," he said, his hand sliding down to the roundness of her ass. A playful glint appeared in his eyes that she adored. "She might get front row seats to a true show out here on the front lawn."

She loved when he relaxed. He was always so serious most of the time, but when he smiled, her heart just melted. She was attracted to his strong, alpha nature, but the soft side of Marcas had her falling in love with him.

Her heart seemed to jump into her throat at the thought.

Love?

Could she be falling in love with Marcas MacArthur?

His lips curved into a smile as he leaned his head toward her. His mouth covered hers in a soft kiss, and she knew she just might be falling for him.

Mac couldn't keep his eyes off Sarena. They followed the restaurant host to their table. Sarena walked in front of him, holding his hand, and they threaded their way toward their table. He sent a glare to a man who was openly eyeing Sarena. He bit back a growl, wanting to lay claim on his woman.

His woman?

Sarena seemed oblivious of the attention. As usual, her outfit was sexy. She'd worn a shirt that hung off her shoulders with a leather mini skirt and heels. Her hair flowed down her back in dark waves, and her makeup was barely there. Mac couldn't stand women who caked on makeup.

Sarena didn't need it. Her natural beauty was what attracted him to her. She was the full package, beauty and brains with a killer body.

"Here you go, best table in the house." The host turned with a smile.

Mac took in the room and appreciated that their booth was placed against the back wall. They could see the entire restaurant.

"It's perfect." He nodded before assisting Sarena into the booth. He slid in behind her. He had chosen an elegant, trendy restaurant that always had a waiting list for reservations.

"Your waiter will be here shortly." The host nodded.

"How in the world did you get a reservation here? The wait list is like months?" Excitement filled Sarena's face as she looked to him.

He shrugged and braced his arm on the back of the booth. "I guess it helps when you save the owner from a situation," he murmured.

Her eyes widened at his comment.

It was the truth. A few years ago, the owner of Lucarelli's, Sergio Lucarelli, was involved in a hostage situation. His daughter, Bella, was with a boyfriend who was deep into drugs and gang life. Sergio's daughter had tried to cut ties with her boyfriend who didn't take too kindly to the break-up and took her hostage and barricaded them into his home, threatening to kill her and him. The boyfriend was coked out and had access to plenty of guns in his residence.

Mac and his team had been called in due to the nature of the situation. Drugs and guns didn't go well together, and they were able to safely extract Sergio's daughter. Because of this, Sergio promised Mac any time he or his men wanted to dine at his restaurant, all they would have to do is call.

"Wow. You know you are a real-life hero." She chuckled, tucking her hair behind an ear.

"I don't do what I do to seek attention." He shook his head. He knew none of his team members desired fame or fortune for what they did. They got called out on a job, and it was their responsibility to ensure all parties lived at the end of the day. Some weren't so fortunate. But it was his highly trained team that was the go-to when things were above and beyond the scope of the regular police officers.

"I'm not saying you do. I don't know what happened with you during your time in the service or even now as a cop, but I hope you do realize that you are a true hero."

He reached out and grabbed her hand and brought it to his lips. He gazed into her eyes and knew he owed her an explanation as to why he was the man he was.

Why he put up walls around himself. It wasn't to protect him.

It was to protect those around him.

"Nurses are heroes, too. It takes a special person to stand up to snarling cops who were brought into the emergency room to be checked over after a bullet hit his vest and not back down from taking care of him," he murmured against the back of her hand.

She scoffed and waved her free hand.

"Declan? He's just a big teddy bear. More growl than bite."

He barked a laugh, thinking that his friend had never been accused of being more growl than bite. He'd be sure to share Sarena's observation with him.

"You should do that more often," she said with a twinkle in her eyes.

"Hello, I'm Talia." Their waitress arrived at their table, interrupting their conversation. She was dressed in the standard restaurant black pants, white shirt uniform. She filled their glasses with ice-cold water from the pitcher in her hand. "I'll be your server this evening. May I suggest a wine for you tonight?"

They listened as she suggested various fine wines their establishment had to offer. His gaze lingered on Sarena while they listened. Her smile was bright as she paid attention to the server.

Once Talia was done with her presentation, he

ordered them one of the limited-edition wines that the restaurant stocked. Talia laid the menu on the table while rattling off the specials for the night before leaving them to decide.

"What should I do more of?" he asked casually, reviewing the menu. He wasn't sure what he had a taste for. The food that came out of Lucarelli's kitchen was prepped as ordered and it was the freshest Italian food anyone could ask for. It had history. Sergio was the third generation to own and run the sought-after restaurant. Everything was made from scratch, and that was why the restaurant was popular with a long wait list.

"Laugh."

13

His gaze flew to Sarena over the menu. She had a soft smile on her lips as she stared across the table. The candlelight highlighted her beauty in the dark restaurant. The atmosphere of Lucarelli's screamed romance and love. Deep down, he knew he wanted to continue showering her with all the things she deserved.

He hadn't thought he would be able to experience these feeling anymore. His little nurse was burrowing into his heart.

"Really?" He cocked an eyebrow at her.

"I love when you smile and laugh. I find it sexy." She tilted her head to the side, waiting for his response.

"Is that an order?"

"Yes, sir."

Desire slammed into his chest for the woman who returned his heated gaze. He reached for his water and took a sip, needing to clear his throat that suddenly went dry. The need to please her was apparent in his chest. He didn't know what it was about Sarena, but he wanted her. Not just for a few steamed-filled, passionate nights, but forever.

The thought had the air escaping his lungs.

Forever with Sarena?

She was a woman that any man would be a fool to pass up.

"Sergeant MacArthur!" a strong voice called out.

Mac turned and found Sergio, the owner of Lucarelli's, headed his way.

"Excuse me," he murmured and stood from the table. "Sergio."

Sergio arrived and engulfed Mac in a tight, manly hug with a few pats to the back.

"I'd thought you would never stop by my establishment." Sergio laughed. He was a large, burly Italian gentleman, who lit up the room with his laugh.

Mac smiled and shook the restaurant owner's hand. "Well, I have an excuse now." He nodded to Sarena.

Sergio's eyes lit up as his attention landed on Sarena. "What a beautiful excuse. Please let me introduce myself."

Mac shook his head. Sergio took Sarena's hand in his and pressed a kiss to the back of it. She giggled, introducing herself.

"I'm Sarena." She smiled. "It's so nice to meet you. I love your restaurant."

"I have been trying to get Sergeant MacArthur and his men to come enjoy Lucarelli's." Sergio turned to Mac and laid a hand on his shoulder.

Mac knew the older man wanted to offer his gratitude for them saving his daughter, but Mac never felt right about cashing in on something that was his job.

"Your meal is on the house."

"Oh, we couldn't—" Mac tried to object, but Sergio cut him off with a squeeze of his hand on Mac's shoulder.

His eyes met Mac's, and he knew when to shut up. The elder man's eyes were locked on him, and Mac got the silent message. Mac had prevented him from having to bury his only daughter. The night they had first met, Sergio was haunted with the possibility that his daughter would die at the hands of her coked-out boyfriend. It had been Mac who'd carried Bella out of the house and placed her into the waiting hands of her father.

"Your money is no good here, Sergeant. I mean it. Enjoy the wine and meal with your beautiful lady."

Mac jerked his head and gripped Sergio's hand in another firm shake again.

"Thank you." He patted Sergio on the back before settling down in his seat as the owner walked away.

"That's so nice of him," Sarena murmured.

"It is," he replied.

Their food arrived even without them ordering yet. He shook his head with a small smile.

Sergio.

They enjoyed their meal and conversation about the action movie they had seen before dinner. Sarena's face was animated, and she argued about the relationship between the hero and the woman he rescued.

"He did it because he loved her," she scoffed.

"So after two dates, he knew that she was the one? To go off, guns blazing across the world to save her?" He cocked an eyebrow.

The movie had been about a cop who was going against all odds to rescue a woman he had just met and slept with once. He snorted then took a sip from his wineglass.

"There is something called instalove." Sarena shook her fork at him then dove into her plate.

He loved that she wasn't ashamed to eat. He was tired of women only wanting salads and picking over their food. He wanted a woman with curves and who could enjoy a real meal with him. He was a large man and loved how Sarena fit against him.

They fit like two puzzle pieces that were meant to go together. Her softness was a direct contrast to his hardness. Just thinking of her soft curves was causing his cock to awaken. He had to will it to settle down.

"So, how does this instalove thing work?"

She paused before putting her food in her mouth and rolled her eyes with a shake of her head. "Men," she muttered.

"What is that supposed to mean? I'm just asking a question—"

The muffled sound of a phone ringing cut him off. Sarena reached down into her purse. Her eyes narrowed on her phone as she glanced at the screen.

Alarms went off in the back of his mind, and he watched her answer.

"Hello?" she said. Her gaze flew to him, and his muscles tensed. "This is she."

She paused and listened to whoever was on the line. Her eyes widened.

"Who is it?" he snapped, not liking the fear appear in her eyes.

"No, I'm not home. Go ahead. I'll be right there." She hung up.

"Who was that?" he repeated, trying to keep the growl from escaping.

"My alarm company. My house alarm was tripped."

"Let's go."

Sarena didn't wait for Marcas to come and open her door to his truck. Her heart slammed against her chest while she replayed the brief conversation in her head from the alarm company.

"Sarena, wait!" His growl echoed behind her as she hopped down from the truck.

She slammed the door and paused, taking a deep breath.

The sight that greeted her left her stomach feeling uneasy. Two police patrol cars were parked in her driveway and street. Their blue and red lights lit up the road. A few neighbors stood on their porches, observing the scene.

Marcas arrived at her side and gripped her to him. "Let me go over and talk with them," he murmured against her head.

"No. It's my house. I want to come, too." She flicked her eyes to his. "I'm sure it was nothing. The alarm probably scared off whoever tried to get in."

The explanation left a bad taste in her mouth. She prayed that she was right. Their neighborhood was a safe one with little crime. It was one of the few neighborhoods that Harden had given his approval of when she'd bought the house.

"Come on." Marcas linked their fingers together and tugged her behind him. They walked across the yard. He pulled his wallet out from behind him and brandished his badge upon approaching the officers as they came out the front door of her home. "Good evening, Officers."

"Sergeant, how are you?" The first one down the stairs met them in the driveway.

Sarena stayed close to Marcas while they introduced themselves. Officers Ross and Sampson were two of the cops who'd responded to the call. They both looked to Marcas with respect when he asked questions. She guessed he outranked them and they wouldn't have a choice. She took notice of the way the officers glanced at her, then down at their entwined fingers.

There was surprise in their eyes, and she bit her lip to keep from saying something inappropriate. She knew instantly what was going through their minds.

"The first floor was ransacked. They didn't get much done, thanks to the alarm system," Officer Ross announced, grabbing her attention.

She gripped Marcas's hand tight in hers. She felt sick to think that someone had violated her privacy and entered her home when she was gone.

"Can I go in?" she asked.

"Please do. We would like to know if anything is

missing." Officer Sampson waved her and Marcas toward the house.

They walked toward the porch with the officers following them.

"We believe they entered through the back door and exited through the front door."

Sarena gripped Marcas's arm as they entered through her front door. She took in her overturned furniture, and her stomach lurched. Not much damage. She walked through the home, taking notice that nothing was missing. All of her electronics were still present. It was like they'd just come in the house and overturned everything.

She was thankful Marcas was with her. He remained calm leading her through the entire house. The second floor remained untouched, just the way she had left it. She bit back a sigh of relief moving back toward Marcas who stood at her bedroom door, silently watching while she had walked around it. She could almost feel the anger brimming in him. His facial expression alone would cause a weaker man to fall to the ground. When her eyes met his, they softened as she made it to his side.

"Are you all right?" he murmured, pulling her into his arms.

She leaned her head against his chest, comforted by his sheer presence. "Yeah. I just feel violated right now. Someone went through my house. My personal space." She fought back tears, shifting her head back to look up at him.

"Ma'am, can you tell if anything is missing?" Officer Ross questioned, jogging up the stairs.

She turned toward him but didn't move from Marcas's comforting embrace.

"No. I can't find anything that is missing. All jewelry is accounted for, my electronics are here. I don't get this. Why break in if you are not going to take anything?" she questioned.

"If you don't mind, we can have you go down to the station for a statement," Officer Ross said.

"No, she will not be going down to the station. She can give her statement here," Marcas interjected.

She felt his muscles tense. Her gaze flew up to his face, and she caught the glare he threw toward the officer.

"Yes, sir." Officer Ross nodded. "Have you noticed anything strange lately around your house or the neighborhood?"

"No, not really." She shook her head.

"Yes. Just earlier today someone stopped by her home this morning," Marcas mentioned.

She had put that event behind her.

"Really? What happened?" Officer Ross pulled out

a notepad and pen. He looked to them, waiting for them to continue.

"I'm sorry. I had already forgotten about that. A gentleman pulled into my driveway this morning when I was returning from my run. He was just looking for another house and had the wrong address. I gave him directions. That was it." She shook her head, not seeing how this could be remotely related.

"Can you describe him, his car, or know the license plate?" Officer Ross asked.

"He introduced himself as Silas. White male, early forties, brown hair, brown eyes, tiny scar on his chin. Tattoo on the side of his neck. I was unable to make it out, the collar of his shirt covered it. He drove a black Audi A7, license plate RGH7483."

She slowly turned back to Marcas, shocked that in that little time, he had memorized that information about Silas. Officer Ross wrote all of the details down on his pad.

"This will help. We'll look into the car and see if we can make anything of it. In the meanwhile, ma'am, you are going to have to get a new lock for the back door—"

"She'll be taken care of," Marcas cut him off, motioning for them to go downstairs. He entwined their fingers together, and they followed Officer Ross toward the front door.

Sarena allowed Marcas to see the officers out while she walked around the living room again, feeling violated. An uncomfortable feeling crept over her at the thought of whoever had been in her house. She righted one of the chairs, trying to keep the tears from falling. At the moment, she didn't feel comfortable staying in her own house. She'd have to call her parents and tell them. She knew her father would demand her to come stay with them.

She brushed the first tear that made it down her cheek. She cursed, not wanting to appear weak, but this scared her. What if she'd been home alone and someone broke in? There was no telling how long it would take the police to arrive.

"They're gone," Marcas announced, walking into the living room. He stalked across and gathered her to him.

"I'm usually not a crybaby," she sniffled, another tear falling.

She bit back a sob as he guided her head to his chest. He murmured words of encouragement, then the gates blew. Sobs racked her body, and she held on to him. His strong hand rubbed circles on her back to comfort her. A few minutes later, her cries quieted, and she tried to regain her composure. She pulled back from Marcas and wiped her face. "I'm so sorry."

"Don't apologize." He tipped her chin back. His

fingers brushed away the missed tears from her cheeks. His dark eyes locked on her. "I want you to stay with me tonight."

"I can't—"

"This is not up for discussion. You shouldn't be alone. We'll close up the back door as best as we can and call a locksmith in the morning."

His face was stern, and Sarena knew she shouldn't but there was no way she was going to argue with Marcas MacArthur. This was one argument she wouldn't win.

"Now, go pack a bag while I go take care of the back door."

She nodded. Not wanting to be alone after something like this, she'd stay with him and in the morning figure out her next move.

14

Mac tucked the covers around a sleeping and very naked Sarena. He paused as she snuggled down into his plush pillows. After they had arrived at his home, they had showered together and fallen into his bed. Sarena needed him, and he was all too willing to meet her every sexual need. She didn't even have to ask, but he knew she needed a distraction from the break-in.

Their lovemaking was urgent, almost desperate. Her body called to his, and he took his time wringing every orgasm from her, leaving her in a deep slumber.

He stared at her sleeping form and gently brushed her dark hair from her face. It had about torn him apart to see the fear in her eyes when she'd walked through her home. If he were ever to get his hands on the person who had brought fear into her eyes, they would no longer breathe. He laid a kiss on her forehead then slid from beneath the covers, grabbing a pair of pajama pants and sliding them on. He picked up his phone and dialed Declan's number.

It didn't matter that it was the middle of the night, he would answer.

"Yeah," Declan growled into the phone.

Mac stepped out of the bedroom. He didn't want to disturb Sarena. After the night she'd just had, she needed to get some rest.

"I need a favor," he began. Greetings weren't needed between them. At this time of night, he knew his friend would know that this was important.

"Anything."

"I need you to reach out to your contact with the Gang Unit." He kept his voice low, walking down the stairs. He didn't want to chance Sarena waking and hearing his conversation. He didn't want to worry her with what he had found in her house.

"What is this about?" Declan went on instant alert.

Mac explained what had happened with Sarena's house. He stepped into his kitchen. Moonlight flowed in through the windows, giving enough illumination for him to make his way to the refrigerator. He flicked his eyes to the time on the microwave and found it a little after two in the morning. He grabbed a bottle of water out of the fridge and leaned against his sink to open the bottle.

"Why would I need to contact the Gang Unit? We can let the regular patrol officers handle a break-in."

"The Demon Lords tagged her house."

Declan released a curse at Mac's announcement. They both knew that the Demon Lords was one of the most violent criminal gangs in South Carolina.

"What connection does she have to them?" Declan asked.

"Not a one." Mac took a swig, but he knew the answer.

It wasn't her, it was him.

SWAT had been called this year to help the Gang Unit with a few busts. The Gang Unit was a small group that was run out of the county's sheriff's department and was developed to investigate all gang-related crimes that were committed by criminal street gangs.

Declan usually coordinated the SWAT team's assignments with the Gang Unit and had grown the relationship with their department and the sheriff's. A couple of times a year, SWAT jumped in to assist the Gang Unit.

Certain gangs were deemed extremely dangerous and required the assistance of a trained team such as SWAT to be involved.

Yeah, the Demon Lords were at the top of the most dangerous criminal gang list in all of South Carolina all right.

Earlier that year, with the help of Mac and his team, the Gang Unit was able to seize a sizable amount of weapons and narcotics that cost the Demon Lords a considerable amount of money. Mac remembered that raid as if it were yesterday. It was a carefully calculated assignment that went to Hell and back fast. Five police officers were shot that night, two being members of his SWAT team. There were countless injured gang members with a few fatalities.

When he'd been helping Sarena clean up, he'd caught sight of a graffiti tag underneath her coffee table that signified the Demon Lords. Someone had taken the few minutes to carve out their insignia there.

When he'd gone out the back to assess the damage to the door, he'd spotted another Demon Lords logo engraved into the wooden jamb. After spotting it, he'd checked the front door and saw the same tag on the upper portion of the heavy oak.

He knew the officers had missed it. He didn't want to alert Sarena to the dangers of who'd truly entered her home. The regular beat cops wouldn't be able to help her.

Her house was tagged, and it meant they would be back.

"Where is she now? She can't stay there," Declan stated.

"She's upstairs sleep." Mac's announcement was met with silence.

"Are you two together?"

"Something like that. Look, she means something to me, man. I'm not sure what, but she does." He let loose a deep sigh. He was in no mood to argue with his longtime friend. He knew Sarena had impressed Declan during their meeting in the emergency room.

"That's all I need to know. I'll speak with Cameron and see what he finds out. I doubt that this is random."

"I know it's not. No way," Mac snapped.

He disconnected the call and finished off his water. He tossed the bottle in his recycle bin then headed back upstairs. There was no way the Demon Lords would be getting their hands on Sarena. The minute he went into the station, they would work on finding out how the Demon Lords knew of Sarena.

The image of Silas in her driveway was the key. He hadn't been lost. Mac was willing to bet he had been sent to scope out the neighborhood and Sarena was just an innocent bystander.

But if Mac was the target, then they had a leak in the station. When SWAT went on gang raids, they all ensured they wore their full gear and masks to keep their identity hidden. Only someone at the police station would be able to identify the members on SWAT, but who?

He arrived back in his bedroom and found Sarena still asleep. He walked over to his side of the bed and removed his pants. Sitting on the edge of the mattress, he reached into the drawer of his nightstand and pulled out his Glock. The cool steel was comforting to him. He placed it on top of his nightstand before sliding beneath the covers.

"Is everything all right?" Sarena murmured as he pulled her curvy body to his.

He breathed in her scent and settled them in the bed.

"Yeah. I just went and got a drink of water. Go back to sleep, baby," he murmured, running his hand down her back. He stared up at the ceiling in the dark and thought of the movie they had gone to see before dinner.

He now had a better understanding of the hero from the movie. Sarena let loose a deep sigh, snuggling into the crook of his arm.

Yes, he understood completely now.

He'd move Heaven and Earth to keep Sarena safe.

"Sergeant MacArthur. How are you?" Sergeant Cameron Kaur met Mac with a firm handshake.

Mac and Declan had driven out to the county's

sheriff's department to meet with the head of the Gang Unit.

"I'm well. Thank you for meeting with us on such short notice." Mac nodded to him.

"Any time. We appreciate whenever you and your men can help us out." Cameron jerked his head to one side, motioning for them to follow him.

They walked through the building until they reached a small conference room. Mac and Declan sat at the table while Cameron sat opposite. They were there to find out information on the last bust they'd assisted with.

They both agreed there was a leak in the department.

"How can I help you, gentlemen?" Cameron asked, pulling a notepad and pen in front of him on the table.

"We have reason to believe that the Demon Lords have tagged a house that belongs to a young lady I know," Mac began.

Cameron's eyebrows rose at the announcement.

"My advice would be for her to move." Cameron chuckled but was met with glares from Declan and Mac.

Mac held back a growl and stared at the sergeant who must have got the message loud and clear. Cameron cleared his throat and turned away from Mac and was met with the same look from Declan.

"I take it the woman in question is someone close to you. But why are they tagging her?"

"Her name is Sarena Rucker, and the only connection to the Demon Lords would be me."

"Declan asked me to gather information on the last time you guys helped us. I brought the files that are not deemed classified. You boys were there so you can piece together what you need."

Mac could remember the last raid with the Gang Unit. It had been a warehouse that had been commissioned by the Demon Lords. SWAT had gone in and secured the premises to allow the investigators to take over. It was not a simple covert mission. A few of his men had taken bullets, and the Demon Lords had lost a few men as well.

The amount of weapons and drugs that were confiscated in the raid was newsworthy. Officers from ATF, DEA, the sheriff's department, and local law enforcement all had to work together. The plan had been executed under the cover of darkness.

That raid had a significant impact on the gang.

"We need to know who was arrested that night, who's in prison, and who is out," Mac growled, catching the file that Cameron slid across the table.

"That night the Demon Lords was almost crippled. We almost knocked out one of the key members of the gang. Cost him almost a million dollars in weapons and narcotics," Cameron said.

"But why would someone target Mac's woman? There were agents from all agencies that night," Declan stated.

Mac opened the file and flipped through the photos of gang members who had been arrested that night as Declan and Cameron spoke. Their conversation faded off in the background, and he paused his hand on one photo and felt the bottom of his stomach give way.

It was the mugshot of the man Mac had trained his MP5 on. The man's malicious eyes that stared at him from the photo were all too familiar. The target had brandished a weapon, and Mac hadn't hesitated in pulling his trigger.

Trevor Tyree had left the raid in a black body bag.

Mac read the list of known associates of Trevor Tyree and let loose a curse.

He now knew why Sarena was being targeted.

"What is it?" Declan's voice broke through Mac's memories.

The leader of the Demon Lords was one Silas Tyree, the cousin of Trevor Tyree.

The man who had been in Sarena's yard wasn't the real Silas. The man had thrown out the name as a warning to Mac. He was just the messenger, and Mac had basically put a X on Sarena's forehead by claiming her in front of him. Had he not come over to them, the messenger would have just hit on her while he was scouting out Mac's home and left.

Instead, he'd gone back to his leader and informed Silas Tyree of something that could be used against him.

Sarena.

Silas Tyree was coming for Mac, and he knew the gangster wouldn't think twice about using a woman to get to the cop who had killed his cousin.

15

Mac was grateful Declan was driving like a bat out of Hell. They had to get to Sarena.

"You've got to get ahold of her and tell her not to go to your house or hers," Declan growled.

"I know. She's not answering her phone," Mac snapped. He hit the disconnect button and redialed her number again. Sarena was at work, and he prayed she would be safe while in the hospital. There were plenty of people around in the busy emergency room.

Again, no answer. Her voicemail picked up. *"Hi, you've reached Sarena. I'm unavailable for the moment. Leave a message, and I'll be sure to get back to you soon."*

He closed his eyes briefly, listening to her sultry voice recording.

"Sarena. It's me. Do not go home or to my house. Go to your parents' house. I'll explain later. Just go to your parents' house when you get off work, and I'll meet you there." He disconnected the call.

"Why didn't you tell her you love her?" Declan asked, his attention focused on the road.

"It would be the first time I've ever said it," Mac admitted, looking out the window. It wasn't like either of them had ever been in a relationship that would warrant emotions and dreaming of a future. "I don't think it would be appropriate saying it on a voicemail at first."

"But you do love her?" Declan glanced at him before turning his eyes back to the road.

They were picking up speed as he guided the car onto the highway.

Mac wasn't sure what love was. He'd never allowed himself to grow close to any female. The only female he'd ever had a close relationship with was his mother.

The vision of Sarena's deep dimples came to mind, her bright smile when she laughed. He was addicted to watching the emotions cross her face when she reached her climax or hearing her call his name while he thrust deep inside her tight channel.

What was love?

If it meant he'd be willing to kill to ensure Sarena was safe, could witness another sunrise, or that he'd have the chance to hold her in his arms again just to watch her sleep, then he'd be the first to admit that Marcas MacArthur was officially in love.

"Yeah, man. I love her. I want her in my life. We are perfect together," he admitted, rubbing his hand across his face. Just saying it aloud was like a weight off his shoulders. He searched deep in his heart and knew that with every fiber in his soul, she was his future.

'I don't care what you've done in the past, I'm the present, and if you play your cards right, I'll be your future.'

Her voice echoed in his head as he thought of how she had burst through his door, her heart on her shoulder. That's what he loved about her. Not only was she smart and sexy, she had a big heart and wasn't afraid of going after what she wanted, and that night, she'd made sure he knew he was what she wanted.

"Let's have a patrolman go to the hospital. Maybe she can't answer, or you know how we can never get reception in some parts of the station," Declan said. "Maybe her phone isn't going off."

"Good idea." Mac nodded, glad that Declan was with him. He was used to being the leader and the one making sound decisions.

"Hey, this is Sergeant Declan Owen. I need a patrolman to head over to General Hospital," Declan ordered.

Mac listened to his friend arranging for the patrolman to go pick up Sarena. The operator put him through to the nearest patrolman to the hospital.

"Officer Thompson, this is Sergeant Owen with SWAT. We are in need of a favor."

A few minutes later, arrangements had been made, and they drove in tense silence.

"Thompson will pick her up. She'll be fine," Declan assured Mac.

"We need to find out the leak. Who in the department would have let Tyree know it was me who killed his cousin? Who would have access to my report?" Mac growled.

"We're going to have to let the captain know," Declan stated. "This needs to be looked into. If they are giving this type of information to the gangs, there's no telling what else was leaked."

"If anything were to happen to her—"

"Don't think that way," Declan cut him off. "She'll be fine. Whoever leaked this will still get an asskicking."

Damn straight they would. Mac's fist would be slamming into their face before IRB could get in their ass.

Mac pulled his phone back out and hit Sarena's name again in his phone. He held it up to his ear, listening to the ringing.

"Come on, baby. Answer," he murmured.

"Hello?" Sarena's voice came onto the line.

He bit back a sigh of relief at hearing her.

"Sarena, baby. Are you still at work?" He glanced down at his watch and saw that it was close to her quitting time. As a nurse, he knew that they never got off on time and prayed this was one of those nights.

"Yeah, I'm still here. What's going on? You sound funny," she replied.

"I need you to listen to me. There is going to be a patrolman coming to the hospital for you. I need you to go with him—"

"Marcas, what's going on? You're scaring me."

"I can't explain now. Just do it. Officer Thompson is his name. He will escort you to your parents' home when you get off. I'll meet you there and I will explain everything as soon as I get there."

Fear gripped Sarena as she packed up for the night. She wasn't sure what the hell was going on, but if Marcas felt she needed an escort to her parents' then so be it. Deep in her gut she knew not to argue with him. Something in his voice had her believing that something was desperately wrong and she'd better do as he'd said.

"Everything is going to be okay," she murmured to herself, shutting her computer down for the night. She was unable to get most of her audits done since the emergency room had picked up with a few traumas that had come in throughout the day. There was no way she would have just stayed in the office while her staff suffered. "I'll have to finish this up tomorrow."

She left her office and closed the door behind her, then walked through the department, waving to her staff as she headed toward the time clock. She swiped out and hefted her bag on her shoulder, tucking her badge into the side pocket. At the sound of her name being called, she jumped.

"Excuse me. Are you Sarena Rucker?" a voice called out.

She turned to see a patrolman standing at the end of the hallway. "Yes, I am." She nodded, butterflies fluttering around in her stomach.

"Evening, I'm Officer Thompson," he announced as she walked toward him.

"Yes. Nice to meet you," she said.

He reached out his hand, and she took it in a firm grip.

"I'm to escort you home," Officer Thompson said, pulling his hand back from her.

"Yes, I received a call from Marcas—Sergeant MacArthur—informing me that I should go with you."

Her hand shook when she pushed her offending hair behind her ear.

He must have noticed her nervousness because he offered her a warm smile.

"Yes, ma'am. I'll get you safely to your destination. We'll take my car, and someone can grab yours later." He motioned for her to follow him.

They walked through the corridors of the hospital leading toward the back entrance that led to the employee parking lot.

"I bet you don't escort women home on the normal." She chuckled, trying to make light of the situation.

"I would say this is actually a perk of being a police officer." He smiled, making her feel comfortable. They shared a laugh, and he held the door open for her. "They did leave this part of the job description out when I joined the academy."

They exited the building, and the night sky greeted them. A patrol car was parked next to the curb, still running.

"So how long have you been a cop?" she asked as they walked toward the car.

"About— What the?" Thomson exclaimed.

Dark figures appeared from behind the bushes and rushed him.

Sarena, unable to let loose a scream from pain

bursting forth from the back of her head, felt herself falling, then darkness claimed her.

16

It had been twenty-four hours since Sarena's kidnapping. Mac growled and leaned back against the wall of the conference room listening to Captain Donald Spook speak about the case.

"Officer Thompson has been upgraded to critical condition. He made it through the brain surgery to relieve the bleeding," Captain announced. "I am being kept apprised of his condition. I've spoken with his mother just a few minutes ago and offered her our condolences."

Nods went around. The air was tense with the thought that one of the boys in blue was hospitalized by a heinous act from low-life gangsters. The entire SWAT team was scattered around the room along with other investigators.

Officer Thompson had been found lying on the ground, having been beaten within an inch of his life. There was no sign of Sarena.

The Demon Lords had her.

It had taken everything Declan had to hold Mac back from turning rogue and going after her. It was Declan who'd forced him back to the station so they could develop a tactical plan to find Sarena.

It had torn his heart apart last night when he'd arrived at the Rucker's home to inform them their daughter had been kidnapped by the notorious gang. The sound of Mrs. Rucker's scream still echoed through his mind. That certainly wasn't the way he'd wanted to meet her parents for the first time. He'd promised the Ruckers he'd bring their baby girl home safe and sound—and he would keep his promise.

"I'm going to turn this meeting over to Sergeant Owen and Sergeant Kaur from the sheriff department's Gang Unit." Captain Spook nodded to Declan who pushed off the wall from his position next to Mac.

He'd have to give his friend some credit. Declan didn't sleep a wink last night. He was right by Mac's side the entire time while they worked with the Gang Unit trying to pinpoint where the Demon Lords could be hiding Sarena.

"Listen up," Declan announced, striding to the front of the room. He and Cameron had scoured it down to two locations that were well-known as hideouts of the gang. Declan stood before the other officers in the room and ensured he met the gaze of each and every one of them. "This is not only just a woman being kidnapped by a gang. No, this is personal. I know we are usually not ones to gossip or call in a favor, but I want you all to know that Sarena is the girlfriend of our very own Sergeant MacArthur. She's one of us."

Eyes shifted to Mac at the announcement. He could see the surprise in his team members' eyes. None of them knew of the involvement between him and Sarena. His team mates moved to stand beside him in a show of support.

He knew without question they'd have his back against anything. He gazed at Zain and Iker who stood beside him and nodded his thanks. He met the gazes of Ashton, Brodie, and Myles and knew his team would be all in for whatever to save Sarena.

Murmurs went around the room. The air became tenser because now this was personal for them all. The Columbia Police Department protected their own. Once word got out, every man and woman who wore a badge would definitely be on the lookout.

"And that's exactly why Sergeant MacArthur should sit this one out," a voice said as the door swung open.

FBI.

"Who the hell are you?" Captain Spooks snapped,

his eyes narrowed on the men who'd entered the room with their FBI-marked blue jackets.

"Special Agent Rhett Gamble." The FBI officer brandished his badge.

They all knew that sooner or later, the FBI would be showing up and trying to take control.

"Special Agent Gamble, my men are the best in the state, and we can handle this. My SWAT team does it all the time," Captain Spooks replied, striding across the room and taking the agent's badge.

"No disrespect to you and your team. I said I didn't think Sergeant MacArthur should be leading the team. He has a personal relationship with the victim," Gamble remarked, his gaze landing on Mac.

Zain and Iker had to hold Mac back when he flew forward with a growl. Chaos erupted as Mac moved across the room. It took three of his men to contain Mac and keep him from reaching the FBI agent. The two agents who were behind Gamble bounded inside as if to stop Mac as well.

"I'm not going anywhere. I will lead my team," he snarled, narrowing his eyes on Gamble.

His men tightened their hold on him. He'd like to see the agent try to prevent him from going after Sarena. No one would keep him from going after his woman.

No one.

"That is a prime example why he should sit this one out," Gamble yelled, trying to hide behind the captain.

"You don't get to decide what my men do," Captain Spook announced, moving away from the FBI agent. "And Sergeant MacArthur will lead his team. Sergeant Owen will be right at his side. I'd rather have Mac somewhere his team can keep an eye on him, otherwise, I'd have to lock his ass up to keep him from going after his woman."

"Captain, I think this would be best discussed in your office," Gamble said, straightening his jacket. He eyed Mac warily, his men releasing his arms.

Mac kept his eyes locked on the agent, his lip curled up in disgust.

"Sergeant MacArthur is the best SWAT officer on the force. He works best under pressure. I can vouch for him since we served in the Navy together. There is no one I trust more than Mac," Declan assured, coming to stand next to Mac.

The other members of the team surrounded them, and they glared at the FBI agent.

"Mac leads," Ashton asserted with murmurs of agreement floating around them.

"Fine. But if anything goes wrong, it's your department's ass that will go down," Gamble stated. "Now let's talk about strategy."

Everyone in the room remained tense as the meeting resumed with Declan and Sergeant Kaur laying out the plans. Gamble refused to turn toward Mac whose attention remained on him the whole time. He knew Declan had devised a well-thought-out plan. By the end of the meeting, everyone knew their role. Since they were targeting one of the largest known hangouts of the Demon Lords, the ATF and DEA were being brought in. There was no telling what they would find. This was the largest raid being planned in the state's history and it was being put together in less than twenty-four hours.

"Any questions?" Declan asked the room from his position in front of the dry erase board. "All right then. SWAT, get your gear and let's roll."

The room hummed with tension while people filed out. Mac felt the vibrations of his phone from his pocket. He pulled it out and saw a blocked number was calling.

"What?" he snapped into the phone. He knew it wouldn't be Sarena's parents. He had ensured they had his number and he'd programmed theirs into his phone before leaving their house last night.

"MacArthur, you better be doing everything in your power to ensure that my sister is unscathed," a deep baritone voice growled.

No introductions were needed. Mac knew exactly who was barking orders at him through the phone.

The infamous Harland Rucker.

"I will bring her home," he promised Sarena's elder brother.

"I just reached stateside and should be in Columbia by nightfall. If you don't find my sister, I will break every known law to go after her," Harlan threatened.

"That won't be necessary," Mac announced, moving out of the room with Declan at his side.

"Make sure it won't be. If something happens to Sarena, you'll have me to deal with."

The line went dead.

Sarena swallowed hard and looked around the room. She had awoken to find herself chained to a wall that was filled with women of all ages. Without even asking, she knew why the women were all chained up.

Sex slave trade.

She'd heard about it in the news and never thought she'd be a witness to it, much less be chained up and possibly sold into slavery.

It had been almost two days since she'd woken up to the horror. All of the women had been kidnapped.

In her short time there, some women had already been taken away and never returned to the room.

She knew she had to stay strong. Marcas would come for her. But then doubt crept into the back of her mind as she thought of their conversation at dinner when he'd refuted her hero comment.

She released a curse as she tried to push down that doubt.

Marcas was a good man. He would come for her. She knew they hadn't reached the point in their relationship where they discussed their feelings. They had been too busy learning and discovering each other's bodies. They were good in bed.

Her heart ached to see him again. She kept the image of him laughing and the intense look he'd given her as he'd guided his cock into her close to her heart.

She knew she loved the intense, possessive man and wished she had taken the time to tell him, even if he didn't want to hear it. She had thought they would have had more time together. Now, she didn't even know if she would live to see tomorrow.

Sarena fought back tears when her thoughts turned to her parents and her brother. She knew what Harden would say.

Fight. Fight with every breath you have until you can't fight anymore.

She was strong.

She would survive this.

She looked around the room again, taking in the young women that filled the space. There had to be about twenty girls ranging in age from teenage up to mid-twenties. They all were tired, dirty, and barely holding on to their sanity.

Cries filled the air as the door flew open. Whenever men came in, a girl was usually taken. Everyone braced themselves to see who they would take this time. The two men, dressed in jeans and hoodies, looked every bit of a street thug. They moved inside, and their gazes landed on Sarena.

She swallowed hard.

They were coming for her.

"Where are you taking me?" she cried out, struggling against them.

They gripped her chains and brought her to her feet.

"Shut the hell up," one growled.

Another clocked her on the back of the head with his fist. She let loose a cry, and stars filled her sight. Her arms were snatched behind her, and tears slid down her face. They handcuffed her and dragged her from the room.

Cries filled the room again as she disappeared. The women knew she wouldn't be back and they would be chosen soon.

"Stand up, bitch," the other one snapped, pulling her arms to where she could get her legs underneath her. Tears continued to flow down her face, and a sharp twinge radiated through her arm. She bit her lip, trying not to show pain or weakness.

They walked down a dark hallway littered with gang members yelling out lewd remarks as they passed them.

"Where are you taking me?" she mumbled, holding her head down.

"I said—"

She braced for another blow, but it never came.

"It's all right, Taser. She wants to know, then we'll tell her," the smaller one cut off the one who had hit her.

Taser's hand gripped her arm tighter, and she winced. She was sure there was some damage done to her shoulder. Pain pulsated from it, and she was convinced it had been pulled out of the socket.

"We are taking you to, Silas."

Confusion filled her, and the image of Silas came to mind. Why would he kidnap her? They'd only had the one run-in before. She bit her lip thinking of what would become of her.

They led her through a door and into a makeshift office. They threw her to the floor. She released a cry, her knees meeting the cold hard slab.

"Here she is, Silas."

Sarena glanced up and froze in place. A chill slid down her spine as she met the cold eyes of the man who sneered at her.

This was not the Silas she'd met.

No, this was not him at all.

17

Sarena's heart raced as she watched the man in front of her move toward her.

"I'm sure you are wondering why you are here," he began, his goons stepping away from her.

"Who are you?" she questioned him. She watched him pace the floor in front of her. "Where am I?"

"I am Silas Tyree." He paused and leveled his cold eyes on her.

"What do you want with me?" she asked.

A smirk appeared on the gangster's face as he turned to her.

"You have Marcas MacArthur to thank for you being here. Because of you, I will be able to get my revenge on your dear boyfriend," Silas snarled.

She shifted her body, kneeling before him. He continued to pace back and forth.

"It was his bullet that killed my cousin, Trevor. Not only did he and the SWAT team cause me to lose almost a million dollars in weapons and cocaine, but he snuffed my cousin."

Horror filled Sarena. She stared at the gangster and had to bite her tongue to keep from defending Mac. She was sure that if he had to pull his trigger on a suspect, he probably did it to save his own life. She dared not verbalized her thoughts by the looks of the crazed gangster in front of her.

She needed to stay alive until Marcas could rescue her.

"He took my cousin's life, and I will take his woman. An eye for an eye. It's such a shame that you would have to pay for the sins of your boyfriend. You are such a pretty little thang," Silas snapped. He leaned in and gripped her chin.

She tried to wrench her face from his hand, but he just laughed.

"Such spunk."

"I know how to break them." Taser chuckled from his corner of the room. "Give me thirty minutes with her and I'll knock the fight out of her."

She cringed with the thought of being alone with the huge gang member.

"I don't think she'd liked that." Silas threw back his head and laughed again before he turned serious. "But I don't give a fuck what she doesn't like. I will give you to my men and let them have their way with you."

"No."

She shook her head as his menacing chuckle filled the air. His eyes narrowed on her, and she knew there was no way she would allow any of his men to come near her. She would fight until there was no breath left in her body. She would rather die than lie down with his goons.

He snatched her face back in his hand and forced her to look into his cold, calculating eyes.

"They wouldn't be loving and kind either like your tough boyfriend. They will fill you with their cocks. You will beg for a bullet after my men are done with you, and you know what? Even then as you are begging for me to kill you, I'll give you to them again," he spat.

The goons in the room laughed and called out lewd remarks of where they'd like to put their cocks.

"You will suffer, Miss Rucker. All because of Marcas MacArthur killing my cousin Trevor Tyree."

He pushed her face away, and she fell backwards. Silas and his goons shared a deep hearty laugh at her fear.

She struggled to right herself on the floor, turning her body on her side and resting on her uninjured shoulder.

She glared at him and prayed Marcas and his men would be arriving soon. Fear gripped her that she may not live to see him again, but she did wish for one thing.

That Marcas would be sending Silas straight to Hell.

The air in the BEAR was tense as the team was driven to the location that they hoped the Demon Lords would be holed up in.

Mac was focused. A strange calming feeling came over him, one that washed through him every time he and his team were dispatched. He would channel his anger into finding Sarena, and the moment he got the chance, his trigger finger would be only too happy to send Silas to the depths of Hell to join his cousin.

Intelligence was coming in that Silas was at the location they were on their way to and this raid would be the 'big one'. It was suspected that there were underage girls being stashed at this warehouse as part of the sex trade. It was also suspected that the gang had gone deep into the sex slave trade. But where there were Demon Lords, there would also be weapons and drugs.

The plan was for them to attack the building under the cover of night. This had to have been the fastest coordination of this kind of raid that Mac had ever seen. All agencies were on board and involved. Not only would they be rescuing Sarena but they would cripple the Demon Lords.

Silence filled the air of the BEAR. The team was deadly and focused.

Declan began going over the plan. "Mac is still in charge. ATF and the DEA will allow us to take the lead in infiltrating the building. They will be right on our asses as we head in. You take down any targets, zip tie them, and keep moving. We have one target to acquire." Declan paused, his eyes meeting every man's in the armored vehicle. "Sarena Rucker."

"We'll get her back, Mac," Ashton announced.

Mac's eyes met his lead negotiator's, and murmurs of agreement went around the vehicle.

"Don't worry, Mac," Brodie said, pulling his mask over his face. "We'll get your woman back safe and sound."

"Just no funny stuff, Mac," Myles's deep voice spoke up. "Grab Sarena and we get out. No rogue bullshit."

Mac turned his eyes to Myles, and his entire team had the same look on their faces. They had read him. His men knew him too well.

"If Silas has harmed one hair on Sarena's head, I can't make any promises," he growled, turning his eyes on his team. He had to beat down the rage festering in his chest at the thought that Sarena had been harmed. "Take her and leave."

Silas Tyree was his.

If the gangster wanted to come after him, for retribution for Mac killing his cousin, he should have been a man and faced Mac. Instead, the gangster had played dirty and grabbed a woman—Mac's woman.

"Fuck, no. Don't stoop to his level, Mac," Zain advised, shaking his head. "It won't be worth it. Sarena will need you. Let the justice system work. The Feds have plenty on him to send him away for a long time."

"We're here," Iker called out from the driver's seat.

The BEAR would be parked a block away with the other law enforcement. They didn't want to alert the Demon Lords that they were near. They would infiltrate the warehouse and take the gang members into custody. The plan was always to do this without loss of life, but in situations like these, the shit could hit the fans quick. Mac and his team were trained for scenarios such as this and were damn good at it.

The Feds had set up in the area and would wait on their signal. Once Mac and his team gave the signal, the other agencies would swoop in and take over.

"SWAT, let's roll," Mac growled as the vehicle came to a halt.

He stood and pushed open the door. Jumping out, he took in their surroundings. His men filed out behind him, grabbing what they needed from the armored vehicle. The other law enforcement agencies were in the area, hidden away, but Mac was able to spot them.

"You good?" Declan asked, coming to stand beside Mac.

Mac jerked his head in a nod. They pulled their ski masks over their faces to protect their identity. He had never been more ready for anything in his entire life.

Mac moved to step away, but a firm hand grabbed his arm. He turned and found Declan's eyes boring holes into him.

"Don't do anything stupid," Declan murmured, keeping his voice low as Iker and Brodie walked by them. "But then again, I know you all too well. Just know I got your six."

"I wouldn't expect you to be anywhere else," he replied, pulling away from his longtime friend. He knew Declan would go to Hell and back with him, but tonight, this was something he had to do alone. He knew how men like Silas worked. Even if he went to prison, he would still run the gang from the inside of his jail cell. If he was gunning for Mac so bad by kidnapping a woman to use her against Mac, then she would never be safe. Anyone Mac loved and held dear would not be safe.

Sarena's smile flashed before his eyes, and he knew

without a doubt he wouldn't be able to live without her ray of sunshine in his life.

"Sync up your communicators," Mac barked, signaling it was time for SWAT to get ready to move.

They each knew their job and would be trusted to execute them perfectly. He grabbed his MP5 from the BEAR and checked it. His body was littered with weapons and ammunition.

This was war.

He turned and found his men waiting for him. They were all decked out in their black fatigues with SWAT brandished across their chests in bright white, weapons in their hands.

"SWAT, time to hunt," he ordered.

18

Mac let loose a curse as bullets flew past him. It seemed as if their cover had been blown the minute they'd entered the building. With their carefully laid plans going to Hell, Declan had called in the other law enforcement agencies to breech the building.

There was no way the Demon Lords would be getting away tonight.

Mac slowed his gait and paused at the end of the hallway and held up his hand. Declan arrived at his side and motioned for the team to hold. Ashton, Zain, Iker, and Brodie lined up behind him with their guns poised ready.

They were deep in the building having made their way beneath the earth's surface. According to their intelligence, the females being held against their will would be in the lower level of the building.

He carefully peeked around the corner. A few thugs ran from a room where feminine screams echoed from. They disappeared around another corner, leaving Mac to go ahead and signal his men to move. In their practiced precision, the back of their line went first. Brodie strode past with his weapon drawn.

Mac waited for his turn as the rest of the team went ahead of him, allowing him to pull up the rear. They made their way down the hallway in tight formation. He moved to the front of the line as they headed to the entrance.

They stormed into the room, and what they found had the bottom of Mac's stomach falling out. He scanned for armed gang members, but there were none. The room was only filled with women chained to the walls. The smell in there was horrid; it reeked of musk, urine, and feces.

Curses echoed around him, and his team slowly crept inside, trying not to scare the women. Brodie and Iker manned the exit as they all took in the women.

"We're not going to be able to stay here long," Ashton remarked, aiming his gun outside the door.

"Call it in," Mac uttered to Declan.

They would notify the FBI where the women were, but as his gaze roamed the room, he didn't see Sarena. He pulled out his phone and brought up a photograph of Sarena that her mother had sent him. He walked around the room trying to find at least one woman who had seen her. Most were too traumatized and scrambled away from him. He growled, trying to hold his shit together.

"Calm down, Mac. These women have been through some shit and don't need another man barking at them," Declan snapped at him, tugging him away from a few who were cowering in their corners.

Mac blew out a deep breath knowing his friend was right. These women would have to wait until the other enforcement agencies could come in and unchain them. The Feds would lead them out of the building safely. He turned and caught a woman with curious eyes staring at him. He slowly made his way to her.

"Have you seen this woman?" he asked quietly, stooping down next to her with his phone out so she could see it.

Her eyes turned to his phone and recognition flared in them. She jerked her head in a nod. Beneath the grime and dirt, she would be a pretty woman. The bags under her eyes spoke volumes. He didn't even want to know what horrors she'd be through. He'd probably lose his shit, just imagining if the same had happened to Sarena in the short time she'd been missing.

"Two of the guards came and grabbed her," she whispered, clearing her throat. Her wide eyes were filled with fear as they flickered around the room taking in his men who were trying to calm the other women down. "She was kept over there. She was a newbie."

"Where do they take the women?" he asked, trying to rein in his emotions. Snarling at her wouldn't get him the answers. She was a victim, just like his Sarena.

"To the boss. Once they go there, they don't come back," she replied with wider eyes.

"Where do they go?"

Her eyes filled with tears, and the floor of his stomach gave way. She shook her head, and the tears flowed down her cheeks. Her lowered eyes had him wanting to unload his clip into a Demon Lord.

He knew the answer.

He released a curse and stood, searching for Declan. He moved to his friend's side.

"They took her from here," he growled.

Declan turned to him and let loose a curse.

A feeling of helpless slowly crept into Mac's chest. "She was here. They're moving her. What if he—"

"Don't think it. We'll get her," Declan barked, his eyes narrowed on Mac. His hand shot out and grabbed Mac's shoulder, bringing Mac back to reality as his imagination tried to run riot. "We'll bring her home."

"Brodie and Iker, you're here with the women until the Feds can get in here. Then you join us," Mac snapped, moving toward the door.

His team mates would follow his lead. It took just

his friend's reassurance to bring the alpha leader in him back to the forefront. He could not lose his shit. Sarena needed him. "Declan, Ashton, and Zain, you're with me."

"Copy that," Iker replied.

With all the commotion going on in the building, Mac didn't want to leave the women unprotected. His men would defend them until they could evacuate them.

"SWAT, let's move," Mac growled, training his MP5 outside the door. He swept the hallway with his gaze before he strode through the door. He felt his team behind him as they filed out in perfect formation.

His eyes narrowed on the hall, and they made their way down it and into the unknown.

Hold on, Sarena, he thought to himself. *Just hold on a little longer. I'm on my way.*

"The Feds are here," Taser exclaimed, moving away from the window in the room. He and the other goon started scrambling around stashing things in duffle bags.

"Your boyfriend thinks he can save you," Silas sneered from behind his desk.

She sat, still handcuffed on the floor, awaiting her

fate. But now with the news that a rescue team had arrived, she hoped she would be saved.

He punched buttons on his keyboard.

Her heart seemed to lurch in to her throat as she thought of Marcas making his way to her. Tears formed in her eyes when she imagined being free soon.

Silas stalked to her and grabbed her by her hair, and she released a cry.

"Come on, bitch," he ground out, pulling her to a standing position, then he and his men made their way toward the exit. He brandished a large gun from the back of his pants and held it pointed at her when they paused at the door. "Smurf, you first."

Smurf? That was the name of the hardened gangster? Her gaze flew to the other goon who leaned out the door slightly.

"The coast is clear, boss," Smurf announced and glanced back to Silas.

"Let's move before the bastards make their way to us," Silas ordered, pushing her out the door behind Smurf.

She stumbled along, holding back a cry.

"We wouldn't want to let your boyfriend see you take a bullet right now, now would we?" Silas hissed in her ear. He kept a firm grip on her arm, guiding her along the hallway.

Taser stalked behind them while they rushed along.

Silas kept the muzzle of the gun pressed into her side, and she bit her lip to keep from crying out. Her arms, sore and achy, were going numb from being locked behind her.

Their pace was fast as they rushed her through the hallways. The sounds of gunshots echoed through the building. She flinched when screams rang out following the sounds of bullets.

They were running through a war zone. Gangsters appeared out of hallways and rooms armed with the guns raised high. They lowered them upon recognizing Silas and his men.

"There are cops and Feds everywhere," one of the new gang bangers announced.

They approached him.

"Is the van ready?" Silas snapped.

"Yes, Loco just drove up." The gangster nodded. "It's parked right out back."

"Hold off the fucking police," Silas growled and dragged her toward the double doors. "No matter what. Don't let them through."

"Just let me go," she begged, but he pushed her out of the building.

Smurf and Taser flanked them, moving across the

parking lot. She frantically took in the dark area, and dread filled her chest. Where was everyone? Shouldn't the cavalry be in the back of the building, too? The sounds of a helicopter met them as it hovered above the warehouse.

"Please. Just let me go. I'll just get in your way."

"Shut up!" Silas hollered, dragging her across the tarmac. "Marcas MacArthur took a member of my family, and I will take away someone important to him."

"No!" She tried to break free, but he tightened his grip on her arm, digging his fingers into her biceps. "Let me go!"

There was no way she could let them put her in the back of the van. She knew if she were to get in that truck, she would never see Marcas again. She didn't know how she would get away with her arms handcuffed behind her.

But she would figure it out.

Silas snatched her from the ground, his arm wrapped around her waist. Her legs sailed through the air, and she let loose a scream, praying someone would hear her. She locked her gaze on the helicopter as it flew overhead.

Please, help me, she thought, continuing to fight.

"You fucking bitch!" Silas snarled. "You're coming with me."

Her body slid down his, and her feet touched down on the ground.

"Let me go ahead and kill her now, boss," Taser growled, pointing his weapon at her.

She stilled at the sight of his gun pointing directly at her head.

Would he shoot her with his boss standing directly behind her?

"Get her in the fucking van. She's our ticket out of here—"

"CPD! Freeze!" a deep voice called out. "Release the girl and put your hands up!"

Sarena could have wept with relief at the thought that her rescuers had found her.

"Fuck!" Smurf muttered as they turned, standing a few feet from the van.

She glued her gaze to her knight in black fatigues. His face may not be visible, but she'd know those deadly eyes anywhere.

Marcas.

19

Mac burst through the double doors with his team right behind him. His breaths were coming fast, and his heart seemed to lodge in his throat when he watched the thug dragging Sarena turn and place his gun to her head. Her eyes were wide as they connected with his. He eagerly took her in. Her clothes were filthy, her hair crazed on her head, and there were smudges of dirt on her face.

Shit.

This situation had gone to Hell in a flaming handbasket.

"Put your hands in the air!" he yelled.

They paused.

His men spread out and aimed their weapons at the gangsters. They all waited for his order to fire. The cop in him was trying to follow protocol, but the man in him wanted to instantly put bullets in the three men who had been dragging his heart toward an unmarked van.

One man sat in the driver seat, waiting on the three thugs to jump in the vehicle. Had they been one minute later, Sarena would have been in the van.

He had to suppress that thought.

His finger twitched on the trigger, his MP5 trained on Silas.

He moved his eyes to the deranged eyes of the gangster.

"Officer MacArthur, nice of you to join us," Silas called out, gripping Sarena to him.

She cried out as he wrapped his arm around her neck and pushed the gun harder against her.

Her eyes widened even more in fear. Tears slid down her cheeks, and she frantically looked to him.

Remain calm, Mac, he chanted repeatedly in his head.

One wrong move, and he was sure Silas would put a bullet in her. Right now, she would be their ticket out of the situation, and going by the sinister grin that spread across the gangster's face, he knew it.

"Why don't you let the female go and we talk like men?" Mac snarled, losing the battle of staying calm.

"Why, so you all can shoot me and my men? Nah, not happening." Silas shook his head.

The thugs next to him had their guns trained on

Mac and his men. He knew they could easily take them down, but he didn't want to risk Sarena.

"I'll tell you what is going to happen," Silas said. "Me and my men will get in the van and will drive off. Once we are safe, maybe we'll talk about an exchange for your woman."

"Not happening," Mac replied, keeping his weapon trained on Silas.

There was no way in hell he would allow her to get into the van with the leader of the Demon Lords. He would never see her again. If she wasn't sold and lost in the underground world of sex trafficking, Silas would surely kill her, just to get back at Mac.

"What do you want?" Ashton, the SWAT negotiator, called out, moving next to Mac. He, too, had his gun trained on the group. Maybe it was best for Ashton to negotiate the release of Sarena.

If they left it to Mac, they'd all be getting shot today.

"Safe passage," Silas responded. His eyes flickered to Ashton.

Mac studied the gangster and knew he could get a shot off, if only Sarena moved to the right just a little. He tried to catch her attention, but she had her eyes squeezed shut.

His heart shattered at the fear that was evident on

her face. If he didn't know better, he'd say she was praying.

"We can do that, but you'd have to leave the girl—"

"Fuck, no! I know you cops. We'd be dead by the time she makes her way to you," Silas said, and his men shifted.

The men didn't relax as they pointed their guns at Mac and his team.

You got that fucking right, Mac thought and was thankful the words didn't spill from his lips.

"We'll give you whatever you want as long as you release the woman," Ashton's calm voice shot out. He lowered his weapon, and Mac knew what he was doing.

Gaining their trust. They wouldn't trust a word he'd said if he kept his gun trained on them.

"Is that so?" Silas's attention was on Ashton.

From their position across the parking lot, Mac could see the thoughts racing in his eyes before they left Ashton and locked on Mac.

"Okay. Let's trade. The woman for Officer MacArthur."

"Deal," Mac growled, not even thinking twice. He'd switch places with Sarena any day.

Her eyes flew open, and she shook her head frantically. "No, Marcus. He'll kill you—"

"Shut up!" Silas hollered, his hand flying to Sarena's mouth. His eyes moved to Mac's as he lowered his gun, and curses filled the air behind him.

"Fuck that, Mac," Declan snarled from his other side.

Mac slid his eyes to look at his friend's.

"Dec—"

"There are other ways," Declan said, keeping his eyes and gun trained on Silas and his men.

"Are you sure, Mac?" Ashton asked quietly, turning to him.

"Anything to keep her safe. The minute she's close, grab her and get her the hell out of here," he snapped, tossing his weapon to the ground. This was going against every procedure code in their handbook, but Mac didn't care anymore. He'd do anything to ensure Sarena was safely returned to her family. "That's an order."

Ashton jerked his head in a nod with his lips in a firm line. Mac could see in his negotiator's eyes that he didn't like the plan.

"Okay. Deal," Ashton called out to Silas.

"Perfect," Silas said.

Mac knew he would have taken great pleasure in killing Sarena to revenge his cousin's death, but to have the man who actually pulled the trigger would be better.

"Remove your mask. I know you have more than

that gun. Toss all your weapons to the ground, then walk ten feet and turn in a circle first."

Sarena's scream was muffled as she fought Silas. Mac held his hands up showing he didn't have any weapon in his hands. Silas gripped her tighter to him, gaining control.

The sound of a helicopter flying overhead filled the air. Mac began doing as the gang leader commanded. He knew it would be minutes before the Feds would be making their way to them.

He kept his eye on Sarena and pulled his other gun that was strapped to his thigh and tossed it to the ground. He removed his helmet and mask, making sure that rage was evident on his face. There was no way he could hide it any longer, and his fingers itched to get around Silas's neck for taking Sarena.

He moved forward and turned in a slow circle to show that he no longer had any weapons on his body. He locked his eyes with the pissed-off eyes of Declan.

No words were needed between the friends. Mac knew Declan would hunt them down the minute the van pulled off. He knew that just putting a bullet in Mac's head wouldn't be as satisfying for the gangster. He'd want to play and torture Mac to make an example out of him. The minute he was in the van, he knew Declan would go after them.

He turned back and faced Sarena and the gangsters. He kept his hands in the air while he made his way to them. He stopped midpoint.

"What are you stopping for?" Silas hollered.

"Trade. Send her over," Mac growled. He wouldn't budge another step until he was sure Sarena was safe.

"Taser, go check him. Make sure he isn't lying about no weapons." Silas nodded toward Mac.

The gang banger named Taser moved to Mac. He braced and stared at Silas as his man came over and patted him down.

"Spread 'em," Taser ordered, running his hands down Mac's legs.

He did as told, not taking his attention off Silas. Taser found the knife strapped to Mac's ankle. He showed it to Silas before tossing it far away from them.

"Nice." Silas nodded.

"Forgot about that one," he murmured, trying to keep his murderous rage down. He swiveled his eyes to Sarena. She whimpered and shook her head. "It'll be okay, Sarena."

"I wouldn't be so sure of that for you, Officer MacArthur." Silas chuckled.

"He's clean," Taser announced, standing to his full height.

"She would have been a good piece of ass, too, but killing you will be even better," Silas said, pushing Sarena forward.

She stumbled, her arms bound behind her.

Mac locked that comment in the back of his mind for later.

"Remove her cuffs. We'll need them for him."

"Marcas—"

"Go to Ashton, baby," he said, not trusting Silas, refusing to take his eyes off him.

The gang leader had his gun pointed to the back of Sarena's head. She moved in front of him. Taser stood behind her and removed the cuffs.

"Go ahead. Give your lover one last kiss." Silas chuckled sarcastically.

"Mac," she whispered.

He flickered his eyes at his nickname. She never called him by it. He preferred her using his first name. The way she always pronounced it gave it a more intimate feel.

Her hazel eyes searched his as he looked to her. "I love you."

He nodded. "I know. I love you, too. Now go," he urged.

She reached up on her tiptoes and gently kissed him on the bottom of his chin.

"Don't go getting yourself killed," she whispered, patting his chest.

He flicked his eyes back to hers and jerked his head in a nod. "I'll come for you," he promised.

"Don't go making promises you can't keep, Officer," Silas snapped. "Let's go. Now cuff him."

Sarena moved from in front of him, out of his sight. He knew that Ashton would come and get her to safety. He walked forward toward Silas, fear no longer lodged in his throat.

Sarena would be safe.

"You got me," he growled, stalking to Silas.

He met the cold eyes of the ganger head-on. Taser moved behind him. He held back a growl as the first handcuff snapped around his wrist.

"I'm going to have so much fun killing you. You won't get as quick a death as my cousin. No, I'm going to draw—"

He didn't get to finish his sentence. Mac pounced. He threw his head forward and connected his forehead with Silas's, cutting him off.

He didn't wait for the gangster to gain his footing again. He went after him in a full-blown act of rage. His fist connected with Silas's face before the gangster was able to right his footing. They circled each other, then Silas swung his fist and missed. Mac would take his anger and rage out on the man who had kidnapped his woman.

He would die in order to ensure she was safe.

Mac knew between the two of them, he could easily take the gang leader, but as he also knew, the gangsters wouldn't fight fair. The other two converged on him, swinging their fists. Mac went down in the fight, taking the hits. As he smacked onto the ground, a boot connected with his stomach. He released a grunt, and the kicks kept coming.

He turned over onto his stomach to get one last look at Sarena as the sound of a gunshot echoed through the air.

20

"Marcas!" Sarena screamed.

Ashton gripped her tight against him as the gunfire echoed through the air. She struggled to be let loose, but his strong arms held her back.

Her body frozen in place, she watched Silas's body go still. A small dot formed on his forehead, a look of horror etched on his face. His knees gave way, and his body crashed to the ground, unmoving.

She turned to find the muzzle of Declan's gun pointed at the melee, still smoking. Declan's hard eyes were locked on the two gangsters standing around Marcas. She gasped and turned back to where Marcas lay unmoving on the ground. The doors behind them burst forth.

The Feds converged on the parking lot. The other gang bangers halted with their hands held in the air. The Feds barked orders with their guns drawn. The scene was like something out of a movie. She took in the throng of people rushing around in the once-empty parking lot.

Sarena broke free from Ashton's grasp. The federal agents surrounded the van and the gangsters, quickly handcuffing Taser and Smurf.

"Marcas," she whispered, watching them being taken away.

A hand gripped hers as she took a step toward Mac. She turned to find Ashton staring at her.

"He's hurt. Let them check him out," he murmured.

Her gaze flew back to Marcas to find EMTs surrounding him.

"I have to go to him," she snapped, pulling her hand away from him. Curses sounded behind her, and she ran forward. She had to get to him. He was willing to give up his life for her. She rushed forward, dodging the crowd of people. Her arms were still aching from being handcuffed behind her, but she ignored the pain as she flew toward Marcas's side.

"Get off me!" he hollered, trying to sit up off the ground. He frantically searched the crowd and relaxed as she made her way to him.

She bit back a smile. He practically growled at the EMT trying to keep him from getting up. He stood to his feet and swayed a little but kept his eyes locked on her.

"Marcas," she cried out, running straight into his open arms.

He grunted and enclosed her in his embrace. She cried, and her body shook with sobs.

They could have lost each other.

"Sarena. It's going to be okay. It's over," he murmured against her ear, gripping her tight in his arms.

She held on with every breath she drew into her chest. She leaned back and met his gaze, and he wiped tears from her cheeks. His face was battered and bruised, but it was handsome face to her and it belonged to the man who loved her.

The man willing to give up his life for her.

"Sergeant MacArthur," a voice spoke up from beside them.

Her body stiffened, and Marcas tensed up at the voice.

"I presume this is Sarena Rucker."

"Yes, it is," he acknowledged, pulling her close.

She turned to find an FBI agent standing next to them. A few other men dressed in the same blue jackets that had FBI sprawled across the chest stood behind him. His cold eyes flickered to her before turning back to Marcas.

"She needs to be taken to the hospital. The EMTs will take—"

"I'm not leaving her," Marcas growled, cutting off the FBI agent.

The rest of the SWAT members encircled them.

"It's all right, Marcas." She tried to rub his chest through his ballistic vest, but it did nothing to calm the rage that was brimming from Marcas.

His murderous rage was locked on the agent. She assumed they had a bad history together, going by the looks they were shooting each other.

"This is exactly why I didn't think you needed to be a part of this rescue mission. You are too close to the victim—"

Marcas moved quicker than Sarena could blink. He had his hand wrapped around the agent's neck. SWAT and FBI moved in, trying to pull Marcas off the FBI agent. She was pushed out of the way during the scuffle.

"Motherfucker." Marcas's curse rang through the air.

Declan and others finally dragged him back away from the agent.

"Control yourself, Sergeant, before I have you thrown in jail for assaulting a federal agent," the man croaked, trying to straighten his clothing.

"Marcas," she called his name, reaching his side again.

His feral eyes turned to her. He shook his men off

and pulled her to him.

"No one will be throwing my men in jail," a voice boomed.

"Captain," voices murmured.

She turned with Mac. A tall man in an official policeman uniform stood there.

"Captain Spook. Your man attacked me." The federal agent straightened to full height.

If the situation wasn't so serious at the moment, Sarena would have laughed at the federal agent trying to tattle on Marcas.

"I demand an apology."

"Get the hell away from my men, Special Agent Gamble, and go do your job," Captain Spook growled.

The agent sputtered but seemed to think twice about whatever he was going to say. The FBI agents turned and walked away.

"You men did one hell of a job," Captain Spook began, facing them.

Murmurs went around as the men all nodded and shifted in place. She looked up at Marcas and felt safe and secure in his arms.

"Captain Spook—" Marcas was cut off by the raising of the captain's hand.

"Mac, go get your woman checked out." Captain Spook nodded to Sarena.

Marcas tightened his grip on her.

"And while you're at it, you get checked out, too. That's an order. The rest of you, I expect full reports on my desk first thing in the morning. Declan, you know the routine. Let's go."

The captain motioned for Declan to follow him. Declan nodded to her and Marcas before he followed behind the captain.

"Thanks guys," she said, looking at Marcas's men.

They acted bashful at her thanks.

"It's no problem," Ashton replied. "We know Mac would go through the same for us. I'm just glad you're safe."

"Keep an eye on her, Mac."

"Always," he replied, bending down and scooping her up.

She cried out, wrapping her arms around his neck. "Marcas MacArthur, put me down. You're injured," she sputtered.

He walked toward the closest ambulance. "Just a few bruises," he muttered then shouted for the EMTs to come check her out.

"I'm fine." Pain in her shoulder made its presence known, and she grimaced. She guessed when her adrenaline had been pumping it hid her pain. The medics brought down their gurney from the ambulance.

Marcas gently laid her on the gurney, his

concerned eyes focused on her as the EMTs surrounded her.

"Be careful with her or I'll punch you in the face," Marcas threatened the medic.

The guy's face grew pale as he looked into the fierce eyes of Marcas.

"Marcas. Let them do their job," she murmured, grabbing his hand and entwining their fingers.

"I almost lost you," he whispered, leaning toward her and resting his forehead against hers. "I'm sorry I laughed at your movie."

"What?" She gasped, confused as to what the hell he was talking about. Did he have a concussion from the fight? "Marcas, what on earth are you talking about?"

"The cop from the movie. True love. I get it."

His serious eyes met hers, and her heart swelled with love for him. He had laughed at the cop in the movie, but now, looking into his eyes, she knew he was dead serious.

He had become that cop. Willing to give his all for her.

She smiled at him, ignoring the medics.

She placed a small kiss on his lips and knew he had gone to Hell and back to ensure she was safe. She'd just have to show him how much his actions were appreciated.

EPILOGUE

Three months later

Mac was manning the grill. Laughter filled the air on his deck. He glanced around and found Sarena and her family enjoying themselves on the patio. As if feeling his eyes on her, she glanced up from her conversation with her mother.

"*I love you*", she mouthed to him.

His heart skipped a beat, and he smiled at her. He threw a wink her way, which made her dimples appear deep her in cheeks as she grinned back at him.

Since the night he and his men had to rescue her from the clutches of the Demon Lords, she'd moved in with him. The past few months had been the best of Mac's life. He finally understood what love was. Just the thought of losing Sarena had him realizing how much she had come to mean to him in such a quick time. He'd learned life was short and one should grab the one they loved and hold on to them forever.

"You doing it today?" Declan murmured, coming to stand by his side. Declan took a sip of his beer and eyed Mac.

Mac had invited his men over for their quarterly barbecue. Some of the guys were in the yard playing a pick-up game of flag football.

This time was more special. He'd invited their parents and brothers over for this gathering. His family had been drawn to Sarena since the moment they had met her.

He'd made the decision to make his and Sarena's relationship official.

His friend had been right all along. Sarena was the kind of woman who deserved a man's last name.

He'd be that man.

He wanted forever with her.

"Yeah," he murmured.

The box in his cargo pants was burning a hole in his pocket. He'd purchased the ring a few weeks ago and needed to choose the right time to present it to Sarena.

Now, seeing her surrounded by their friends and family, he knew this was the right time.

"Watch my six," he murmured, putting the spatula down and moving away from the grill.

"Always," Declan replied immediately. "But right now I'm going to watch these burgers," he muttered behind Mac.

Mac locked his eyes on Sarena and made his way across the oversized deck.

"Sarena." He cleared his voice.

She turned her eyes to him and smiled up at him, tilting her head back as he stood next to her chair. His heart was racing a mile a minute. He'd never been so nervous before a day in his life. He reached for her.

"Hey, baby. What's up?" she asked, laughing when he pulled her up from her chair.

He could feel everyone's eyes on them as he gathered her to him. Her body instantly molded to his as it did every time. They were a perfect fit.

"I love you," he murmured, staring deeply into her eyes.

The music was lowered. She returned his gaze. He reached up and brushed her hair away from her face.

She would be his future.

"I love you, too. Marcas. What is going on?" She gave off a nervous laugh and looked around to see everyone had stopped what they were doing and observed the two of them.

His men had shit-eating grins plastered on their faces.

"You're acting weird."

He glanced at her parents, and they nodded to him. A week ago, he'd met with them behind her back and asked for her hand in marriage. He'd even had the talk with her brother, Harden. Knowing he had the blessing of her family and best friend Ronnie, he was going to do the one thing he never thought he'd ever do.

He got down on one knee.

"Marcas," she exclaimed, her hand covering her mouth.

He brandished the small black box in his hand. Tears welled up in her eyes as she realized what he was doing.

He opened the box, revealing the three-carat ring. "Sarena, marry me." He didn't need a long, drawn-out proclamation of love. Every day he had made sure she knew he loved her. She meant everything to him, and he wanted to bind her to him forever.

The tears fell down her cheeks, and she nodded. Hooting and hollering from their friends and family filled the air, and she held out her hand to allow him to slide the ring on her finger.

It fit perfect.

He stood and wrapped his arms around her, and her body shook. He tilted her head back and wiped the tears from her eyes.

"You're crazy, you know that, right?" She laughed,

reaching up and entwining her fingers at the base of his neck.

She was the most beautiful woman in the world to him. Her bronze skin practically glowed as she stared up at him.

"Crazy over you," he murmured and proceeded to cover her mouth with his.

The End

A NOTE FROM THE AUTHOR

Thank you for taking the time to read Dirty Tactics. I hope you enjoyed Mac and Sarena's story! If you love this book and want more from this series, please leave a review!

Reviews help authors know reader's reactions and that you want more from us! Thanks in advance!

Warm wishes,
Peyton Banks

ABOUT THE AUTHOR

Peyton Banks is the alter ego of a city girl who is a romantic at heart. Her mornings consist of coffee and daydreaming up the next steamy romance book ideas. She loves spinning romantic tales of hot alpha males and the women they love. Make sure you check her out!

Sign up for Peyton's Newsletter to find out the latest releases, giveaways and news! Click HERE to sign up!

Want to know the latest about Peyton Banks? Follow her online

ALSO BY PEYTON BANKS

Current Free Short Story

Summer Escape

Interracial Romances (BWWM)

Pieces of Me

Hard Love (Coming 2018)

Dirty Tactics (Special Weapons & Tactics 1)

Dirty Ballistics (Special Weapons & Tactics 2) (TBD)

Mafia Romance Series

Unexpected Allies (The Tokhan Bratva 1)

Unexpected Chaos (The Tokhan Bratva 2)

Unexpected Hero (The Tokhan Bratva 3)